THE FATHER

A NOVEL

Andrés Cruciani

TOHO

PUBLISHING

Copyright © 2017 by Andrés Cruciani

All rights reserved. Published by Toho Publishing LLC, Philadelphia in 2018.

FIRST EDITION

Cover by Bia Andrade

ISBN 978-0-578-42924-3 (paperback)
ISBN 978-0-578-42923-6 (ebook)

www.andrescruciani.com

AUTHOR'S NOTE

Dear reader: the book that follows contains some dark themes that may be stressing to some. I can't predict how you will react, but I wanted to let you know that while I haven't harped on the traumatic, I have attempted in this work to paint a slice of the world not as it could be, but as it is. In this painting, there is both beauty and love, and tragedy as well. I neither glorify nor condone. I have simply tried to create a work of art—flawed, imperfect, difficult. Ultimately, this painting is simply one of a tiny mirror.

I

♠

The story I'm about to tell is a bit of a strange one, and by the end of it you might be wondering, as I did, what the moral was. But it kept me glued to my barstool all evening and night. Patrons came and went, interrupting to ask questions and then to add they didn't believe the answers, but mostly the story ran like a reservoir's overflow, building from a life's downpour and draining just this once. At least that was the impression our storyteller gave. He went by the name of Savage.

I'd been sitting in a bar with a friend of mine, Augustin. The bar was mostly empty because outside it was sunny. But on this particular day, I was in a particular mood which Augustin called "grim about the mouth". I had recently lost a close friend, Alfred St. Mary, and had also recently finished writing a novel. I was mourning both—Alfred deeply, but the novel perhaps more so for I had nothing to fill my idle hands with. It was turning out I could live without relations but not without a purpose.

Anyway, I was explaining exactly that to Augustin. He's large and big eared and works in sales, and I was unburdening my writer's woes when his platitudes began to feel like stabs.

Finally, "Listen," he said, "you'll write another book."

"You don't understand."

"Look," he said, putting down his bourbon. "Just make stuff up. Jesus, you're sitting there with a pen staring out a window while other people are out there actually working—"

"What?"

"Come on. People are out there starving and slaving in factories, losing life and limb just to make that pen you hold. Meanwhile here you are complaining that writing's hard."

I stared at him.

He took a gulp and coughed. "What."

"You're just a salesman."

"So what."

"So is that God's work you're doing? What was it Priscilla said?"

He stood up. He rummaged his pocket and tossed a crumpled twenty on the bar. "I told you that in confidence."

"No, come on. You said that she got fat because you did, but now you think you're better than her. Do nothing at your job and then—"

He grabbed my arm, spilling some of my beer. "I was trying to help you."

"Don't," I growled and listened as he walked away. "Augie," I called out, but when I turned, the door was already shutting.

♤

Avoiding eye contact with the bartender, I mopped up my spilled beer. I sat stewing, but soon I started planning my apology. If I hurried to catch him, maybe he'd forgive me.

I was standing, leaving a tip, when a man from the end of the bar waved.

"You're a writer," he said.

I threw my bag over my shoulder.

"Hold on," he said.

I looked down the bar trying to make him out. He was silhouetted by a dark, dirty window. He was large and bald and dressed in a black shirt with only one long sleeve.

"Are you a writer." He made statements of questions.

"Yes," I said.

"Well I have a story for you."

"I have to go," I said, for I was on the verge of losing another friend, this time not to an air conditioner's cord but to my own stupidity. "But here's my card." I reached for my wallet.

"I asked if you were a writer. You said yes."

The bar door opened and cast him in a shaft of light: not bald but head shaved, not a long sleeve but an arm tattooed black. His eyes twinkled.

"The writer's profession is a sacred one," he continued as the door shut. "In the beginning was the word. Book of John. And you've chosen to make a career from that which is holy. So it falls upon you to keep it so. To transcribe God—regardless of whether His words stoke war or love—for your purpose is not to parse but ruin should it be so deemed. Not to hem by censorship, obfuscation, or apology, but to lay down the very commandments, saying, Do as you must, for I have been conduit to His will. And if my reward is fame or death so be it."

His beer sat untouched as though he'd come with one intent but stayed for another. He continued:

"I once read of an old fool who said that when he wrote he was like an antenna, his hand just annotating what his head picked up. Even on his deathbed he refused to acknowledge God though that's whose voice he'd been taking notes on his whole life. The proud fool. Too big of an ego to know the bigger one above." He looked down at the bar. "Do you know this voice."

I dared not call it God's, but, "Yes," I said.

"Good," he said and pushed the stool out beside him.

♤

His words struck me with a profundity I'd not felt since Alfred's funeral when from the pews I'd sat listening to his estranged father's eulogy. A speech filled with remorse for decades ago, having little character or wealth, he'd concluded his son Alfred better off without him. This he confessed to those of us who had been there, who'd delivered Alfred to the psych ward and nursed him. His father speeched, said that all he'd done was to rationalize his own selfishness, and that only now, looking at his dead son, could he acknowledge what he'd always known: he was wrong. Too late. The last time they'd embraced Alfred had been a child. I sat there watching his father blubber through this written speech and though I'd been the one to find Alfred dangling onto the courtyard behind his apartment building, a sparrow chirping from his shoulder, though I'd cut him loose and watched him tumble down fire escapes to land contorted on a vegetable garden, had straightened his limbs and shut his eyes, I wished his father's pain on no one.

I took the stool, pulled out my notebook and recorder, and ordered a whiskey.

"Ok," I said.

The man stuck out his hand. We shook.

"Savage," he said.

"Is that your first name or last?"

"Just Savage," he said.

♤

He was born and raised in the southern town of Kitty Hawk, North Carolina. A seaside town of fishing and strip malls that swelled with tourists in the summer and contracted by winter when vacation homes emptied and shops shuttered. A seasonal breathing.

He attended small schools on that island strip called the Outer Banks, home to Kitty Hawk—best known for the year 1903 and brothers Orville and Wilbur Wright. He'd often visit the site of their first flight, since turned national park, and stare into the mockup of their cabin. He'd pace the markers of their famous flights and with his bicycle propped beside him, he'd spend afternoons lying by that final marker, Wilbur 852, feeling the ocean breeze and watching gulls circle, reveries which led him not to aviation but to the thought that he was destined for greatness.

His father was a mechanic and his mother a teacher, and they loved him and his sisters. His father once shot, skinned, and gutted a maimed deer in their front yard and his mother slapped him for trying on his sister's dress, but as far as he could tell, there was nothing in his childhood to explain the man he'd become. Except perhaps for his senior prom.

He'd carried his prediction of greatness throughout adolescence, and it had pushed him to challenge himself despite a body and mind proving themselves average. He'd fought to be in honors classes only to do poorly. He'd competed in the discus against two-hundred-pound football players to predictable results. Yet when it came time for prom, he still decided to ask the girl he thought the prettiest in the whole school, Sarah Banter. They'd spoken less than a spider leg's worth, as his father would say, but he had on his favorite knee-torn jeans and jean jacket when he stopped her outside of chemistry class.

She was something sprung from a dream. Recounting that day he thought he only remembered the story of a memory—the freckles, the red hair and gemmeous eyes not even an after-image but something dim and gone.

He stuttered his proposition, cleared his throat, and tried again. "Would you go to the prom with me?"

It was not the admission of infatuation he'd rehearsed, but it didn't matter.

"Yes," she said.

Prom arrived and with his father's jalopy still running, its passenger door open, he rang her doorbell. Doubts arose. Accustomed to failure but each time by it offended, he could not believe that she'd agreed—that her father wouldn't answer the door to tell him she'd already gone with someone else. His sweaty hands were slicking the plastic box of a corsage and he was scanning the yard for a suitable bush in which to throw up when the door opened.

"In a prom dress to enrage Aphrodite," he retold.

Shy at first but soon loosened by the flask of rye he'd stolen from home, they danced and laughed and when the prom was over he swerved them to Avalon pier where people were gathering for a bonfire. He laid a blanket on the sand and under a tarp of stars they watched others frolic round the flames and they shared what remained of the whiskey and he had his first kiss. To waves crashing and moonlit foam sizzling, they watched others doff their cheap tuxes and dresses to run naked into the dark water. And soon her friends returned, dripping, immodest, and giggling, to drag Sarah to her feet. Slapping them away at first but finally with a happy shriek consenting, she stripped to what he'd only seen in magazines and an unintentional glimpse of his mother. With Sarah's dress crumpled in the sand, "Come on!" she shouted as she ran screaming, her white figure disappearing behind the bonfire into that dark expanse beyond, but with no one to goad him, he watched and waited, and then, with an unclipped bowtie dangling from his hand, he stood and waited, and soon they all screamed and screamed, but she never came out.

♠

I wanted to tell him about Alfred. To tell him that
life is a strange phenomenon to which we
accustom. If before our births our spirits choose
the lives we'll lead, or if we repeat this same life
infinitely, regardless we forget our pasts and live
in a bourgeois alliance between perception and
magic. We forget the miracle of our existence
and come to expect it.

The ice in my whiskey cracked, and I wanted
to tell him I had no idea why I'd chosen this life.
I felt an incredible loneliness and that love was
simply that solitude's abatement: a surfing of
this terrifying tide together. Loneliness
subsiding. The inward eye turning out—but then
death returning as a reminder. Yet I said none of
it. He looked at his full beer and wiped an eye
with a finger on which her name was inked.

"I haven't even gotten to the kidnapping," he
said.

His unpronounced love for Sarah had been a
flower's bud. A potential, ideal and imaginary,

against which no future love could compete.

With a sewing needle and ink, he'd tattooed her name on his finger: Sarah. He learned to hide it when necessary, but he would find that with his hand just so, the finger was a lure. They would ask who she was. I'm so sorry, they would say. And he would learn sadness and pity aphrodisiacs.

With his finger tattooed, he swore he'd never love another.

His high school graduation was uneventful until a peer, Kevin Splaner, drunk on moonshine, streaked across the football field. A hundred heads turned from the stage to watch Kevin sprint straight into the goal post. A communal groan. An ambulance. Months later you could find him on Route 158, picking up trash and wearing a sign: I'LL DO BETTER.

Savage worked that summer in a hot dog stand, but still convinced destiny had greater in store, he stuffed his backpack and bought a bus ticket to New York City. With the wind blowing in from the Atlantic, it was dog-nose cold the night he left.

♤

The ride from the bus depot in Elizabeth City, North Carolina, to New York is eleven hours, which is long or nothing, depending. Savage had been neither north of Maryland nor south of Georgia, so to him it was eleven hours into a new country. His resolve had taken his every ounce of courage. He had stayed up nights debating, thrilled, terrified.

Yet once he'd decided—and left with his sister, as insurance, fifty dollars for a return trip home—fear and uncertainty dissolved. Heading north, watching dark fields whose cotton bolled like stars, he tried to take it all in. To sear into his brain a crumbling chimney in a grass field, last remnant of a bygone plantation, to imprint an image of a boarded house spray-painted with DO NOT TRESPASS. YOU WILL BE SHOT, and as he looked out, he remembered his father standing at the door as he left, saying: "Son, I was once in your shoes. You are breaking your mother's heart, but that's what mother's hearts were made for. So go do what you must, but for the next two years, you have no home here. You understand, boy?" And then his father thrust out a handful of small bills and closed the door.

♤

Savage cleared his throat and took a sip of beer surely warm for he'd been cupping it. He wiped his mouth and, "I loved that man," he said. "He was tough, but he always tried to be more than he was."

Twenty years of southern comfort and beach living came to an end as he stepped off that bus into New York City and headed up the terminal's stairs. Lights, billboards, bars, restaurants and homeless and he stooped beside one and said, "What do you need, friend."

The ravaged man replied: "Five dollars."

Savage gave it to him.

Then, "I need another ten," said the man, and Savage gave him that too.

But of his first day, what he remembered most was the dawn, a sun like a golden coin.

He walked north the miles from midtown to the Bronx where he'd arranged a hotel room by telephone. Traversing that city, he felt foreign. He'd graduated with a class of thirty, had known the names of not just the mailman and pizza delivery boy but the garbageman too. Yet this— the shouting, the honking, the cursing and panhandling and prostitutes, the heckling by daybreak—it was a miracle, a thing he'd never again experience in the same way as when he'd plodded wide-eyed and slack-jawed under his heavy backpack, not mugged out of a communal pity. Give this fish a few days.

♤

He arrived at the hotel three hours later, guided by the memory of the directions he'd forgotten on his desk.

"Ma'am, I'm looking for the Hotel of the Virgin of Guadalupe," he had said to an old woman.

"Sounds bad," she'd replied.

The hotel was a rowhouse. Rundown, peeling, rust streaked. He climbed the stairs and rang the bell. The door buzzed open. He pushed on the graffiti of a grated window and entered a lobby remarkable only for its smell. No one was behind the counter, so he sat in a rickety plastic chair and waited. A half hour had gone by when the doorbell rang and he heard a snort.

Savage stood and headed to the counter. He looked down. Someone slept on a cot.

"Sir," said Savage, "I booked a room."

The man grumbled. An arm slung over his face. He rolled over to push the button that buzzed the door open. Eventually he stood. He was gangly, his eyes sunken.

"How long," he said.

"I spoke to someone over the phone, sir. Two weeks."

The man nodded a greeting to the resident just entered and then he took out a ledger and a key from the wall behind him and said, "You pay up front." He penciled some math. "Hundred twenty six," he said.

Savage feigned braveness. "No, sir. I was told five a night over the phone."

"That was then. It's nine a night now." The man pointed up at a handwritten sign hanging beside a cheap icon of the Virgin Mary.

Savage looked down at the ledger's long list of signatures. Many signed with an x. He thought about how much money he'd have left. Then he clenched his jaw and signed and from a wad of bills counted some out. The man watched.

♤

He lived off crackers, tuna fish, beans. The biggest purchases he made were of a can opener and a portable radio bought from a man selling junk on the sidewalk. Yet to the newly initiated into independence, this was adventure. The dark, moldy, bug-infested room he called home. At night he'd listen to the radio and write letters and he'd fall asleep to shouts and sirens and gunshots.

He spent his days looking for work. Traipsing Manhattan and sifting newspapers and soliciting stores, restaurants, bars. One day he stood in Grand Central and asked everyone who passed by for work. He did not get a job, but he did learn something: the urgency of our own lives blinds us to the needs of others.

Yet he was not dispirited. In fact, he appreciated his plight the more. Even on a cold spring evening when trekking home, down to his last ten dollars, a hooded man lunged from an alley and mugged him at gunpoint—took his boots and jean jacket and he had to go on home in his socks—even still he did not lose heart, for he felt he had a guiding star. Fate or God's own intent goading him onward, testing and embracing him at once. When a few blocks from the hotel he saw sneakers hanging from a tree, he knew they'd fit. And they didn't smell too bad either.

He was wearing them the day he returned to the hotel with his meager groceries and not a nickel remaining when the manager stopped him.

"Sir, I paid another week."

"No," said the manager, scratching himself. "You paid four extra days."

Savage looked at the wall behind the counter. The keys hanging. All those empty rooms.

"I need to get my sleeping bag," he said.

The manager shook his head. Bits of dandruff fell.

Savage looked him in the eye.

"God don't like ugly," he said, and left.

♤

He had lost his radio and his sleeping bag and the can opener, but he was fortunate to have gotten into the habit of carrying his backpack with him—this after he'd seen a middle-aged woman tossed from the hotel, escorted out by police as she screamed.

Fortunate too did he consider himself that though his sneakers buckled, their soles and laces were strong. That they were not his made him feel of a part with the city. Nothing new, everything swapped, call yourself of it when everything you have is another's.

He walked the miles down into Manhattan and he found a small park with a bench obscured by a tree and using his backpack as a pillow he lay there curled beneath his only sweater and he listened to traffic and the occasional clip-clop of wooden heels. He did not bemoan his lot but felt that his life had finally begun. Though he had no money and his shoulder ached from the slats of the bench, he smiled at the slender moon hammocking the sky above and fell asleep.

He awoke a few hours later to his stomach grumbling and he cranked open a can of beans with the knife he carried and he ate.

The next day he was hunting for work when the bartender of a small bar told him he'd better leave his backpack outside while he inquired because it made him look homeless.

"I don't have work for you," said the bartender in a vague accent, "but clean up yourself in the bathroom."

Savage locked the door behind him and when he turned the light on he jumped at his reflection. He was gaunt. His hair was oily and his face dirty. He smelled. He took off his t-shirt and with a sliver of soap washed himself and then he put his shirt back on inside-out.

The bartender slid him a half pint of beer, and after Savage had guzzled it, he filled it again and scrawled an address on the back of a coaster. "They don't pay good and they don't treat you good, but it's money," said the bartender. He refilled Savage's glass.

♠

He worked as a bar-back at a touristy bar. Long hours, low pay. But the manager paid him the first day and then weekly after that, and soon Savage could afford his own apartment in Harlem. Tiny and with a shared bathroom, but it was his.

At the bar he met women. His dimpled smile, his Southern courtesy, the story of his tattoo—lures for the old, young, moneyed, foreign, seductive, tactless, beautiful, dull, a veritable buffet ... And he'd been shuttling dirty glasses past his white-haired louse of a manager when he heard her name: Sarah.

He turned round and saw two young women talking and guessed correctly which one was her. Her skin was the color of mahogany and she had pitch eyes, curly hair, and glasses. He stood before them pretending to work and eventually they enjoined him in conversation and not long after the other woman left but Sarah stayed, drinking gin and tonics and reading a book she'd tell him about later as he walked her home.

She was a sophomore in college and she lived
with three other women and when they arrived
at her apartment she told him to wait and closed
the door. He stood in the building's hall trying to
name its strange smells. When she opened the
door again she grabbed him violently and drew
him through the dark toward the candle-lit
couch she'd fitted with a sheet. They groped and
disrobed and he thrust into her wondering if this
was the consummation of a love begun with
another. If this Sarah would die too. Gyrating
under the soft light she saw the tattoo he'd kept
hidden and her eyes grew wide. Black oases.
Later she woke him: "Who is she?"

In the morning the two laid on the couch as
her roommates primped and readied themselves
and from an impetus he could not guess she told
him this: "You'll always love her more. I
shouldn't see you again."

♤

Savage stood. "I need a cigarette," he said.

"I'll join you," I said.

"No." He fished in his pocket.

The bar door opened onto daylight and shut and I was left alone until the bartender snapped me from my reverie.

"What?" I said.

"When's he gonna get to it?" He passed me a filled beer. "The kidnapping."

I shrugged.

"Well, I hope it's soon. Too much foreplay. Sometimes you just gotta get it in."

♤

It was the serpent's tail of summer. Savage was working the early shift, prepping the bar, when she returned. Less pretty than he remembered but more alluring. The bar was closed but she entered and sat anyway.

"What time are you done?" she asked.

"What day is it," he said.

"Tuesday."

"Early then," he said. "Midnight." He held a box he'd brought up from the basement.

"I'll come back," she said, and him too slow with his rebuttal, she left.

He waited for her, but she did not come that night or the next. No phone number and a forgotten address.

Once, he tried to return from memory, but unable to find her building, he spent the evening sitting on a stoop, watching others pass.

He thought of her often. As he ate. As he held others. He was a man distracted.

Weeks later, he was locking up when a hand grazed his shoulder.

"Where've you been," he said.

"I told you I'd be back," she said.

Her face reflected the city as once more he walked her home. He studied her gait and how her eyes settled on him: warm, calculated.

They stood on the stairs to her building but she would not let them kiss.

"I moved too fast," she said.

She turned to unlock her door.

"Wait." He tried to stop her. "Give me your phone number. You can't just—"

But laughing she shut the door.

He stood there until he heard tapping. He looked round and then headed to the sidewalk and then he looked up to see a nude figure in a window disappear behind a snapping curtain. He did not know then: she was tossing him back to sea, unspooling line, waiting for him to jump back in and offer his gills. He felt helpless. Clomping home in his new boots, he was wild— elated and enraged both

He did not sleep. She did not return.

When a week later she did, he grabbed her.

"You can't keep doing this."

She smiled. "Well, you have a choice. You can have my number now and I'll leave here alone. Or you can walk me home again.

"Both."

"Choose," she said.

He calculated.

They walked slowly and told each other their lives. She'd been raised in Georgia and transplanted to New York. She studied English despite her mother's disapproval. He'd once been cut by a stingray and his youngest sister, Mary Anne, cried as she played the piano. When they arrived at Sarah's steps, they stared at each other and her stoop light cast them in sharp relief.

He looked down at his boots, then up.

"Not again," he said, but she was already unlocking her door.

"I love you," she said and shut it.

♠

It's hard to make a grown man listen to a story about young love. It can arouse disdain, apathy, even envy, but when told sincerely, it can also invigorate that which all have had or aspired to: love. It can arouse that deep desire to be cared for, perhaps strongest but hidden in the hardest among us who spend lifetimes constructing their own cells, inwardly crying: love. These stories of innocent love requiring no more than proximity or a look—no melding of minds but simply a thunderous clap—such stories can arouse those tender feelings that dissipate with the birth of ambition, can return us to a time when love was indeed enough, and can inspire in us that comorbid compassion, which we then actualize on the story teller before us. And though I, like the bartender, wanted our raconteur to get on with it, such is the compassion with which I looked at him, our Savage. He took a swig of beer.

"I mean, imagine you're nineteen, the love of your life dead before you can tell her how you

feel because you're too young to know it—love—
and even if you did you mightn't've had the
courage to name it so. And the wound still
tender, the moment you realize you've deigned to
love another, she disappears.

"There you are requiting her gift in kind,
putting yourself on the line with those three
words some never say: I love you—able to
pronounce hate smugly but try telling a stranger
you love them—add to that the fact you've only
ever said it to kin, and it feels like those words
are a noose and the only way to be freed of it is to
hear their echo. And yes she said it first but then
she shut the door and disappeared. Three weeks.
And while that might not seem long to you, when
you're nineteen, three weeks is to your life what a
year is to a centenarian—the difference between
animation and death—and every feeling you have
is amplified by inexperience and you feel that if
you do not see her again and perform the deed at
which that love we've diminuated to call puppy is
aimed, you will go mad from the pressure—you
are like a schizophrenic or a boozehound with
the DTs, a loon. You cannot eat sleep nor drink
and the only thing returning you to work is that
you've accustomed to sleeping in a bed under an
actual roof. Working day in and out despite the
fact that you cannot think. No thoughts, just a
mad rush of unreined emotion. Your eyes are red
with love and if you do not find recourse you will
kill. You become violent and quick-tempered.
Though your job hangs by the thread of your
manager's whim, you snap at him anyway, and

the women that had previously streamed, they run dry. A man in heat knowing no recompense even as he stands before his lover's building howling under a full moon because you've become a slave to the passions ignited by a woman practicing dark arts of which you've never dreamed, had always imagined love a genteel affair but now here you are shouting her name—Sarah! Sarah!—having forgotten which window was hers. Raving like a lunatic for the nineteen-year-old vintage she's uncorked but stopped up again by saying, Not yet, Not yet, leaving me to froth. And if she'd followed the steps of my first Sarah into the sea or if she'd fallen beneath the wheels of a truck I did not know. I was left boiling atop the flame, spattering and spitting until after three whole weeks of fiery delirium, she finally showed up and the first words out of her mouth were: I'm pregnant."

♠

She moved in with him soon after. There was no talk of abortion for it was like they both knew: to abort the child was to abort their destiny. Unsaid but, like weather, felt.

There was a wisdom to her whose source others might have guessed the books she crammed into their apartment but that Savage knew sprang from within, innate. So when she said, "Let's wait till it's born before telling our parents," he agreed. And on those rare occasions when he called his family, he made no mention of the pregnancy, or her.

The weather cooled but their apartment warmed by the blankets she'd brought, by the scarves she knit and the meals he prepared.

One evening, she was organizing their small kitchen when he kneeled beside her.

She smiled. "Do you really think you can take a vow you'll stick to for sixty years?"

He did not hesitate. "Yes," he said, opening the box of a cheap ring.

"No," she said.

He closed the box. "I don't understand."
She lowered to him. "No," she repeated.
Still, they built their nest.

Now, had she agreed, their futures might have been different. Forced by vow's shackle, he might not have done what he would. But she rejected the binding of their intents. And while perhaps she'd thought it a noble, modern gesture, it had forced him to restrain that part of himself that held purity and promise as virtue. Denied, it morphed.

THE FATHER

♤

The weather grew colder and the days shorter yet still she studied for school and he worked for the expenses he knew would arise. He gave up drinking and, despite his late shifts, did his best to maintain a normal schedule. He prepared her breakfast and they would sit on their window sill eating eggs and grits, watching commuters traipse through foot-high snow.

Finally, with winter past and pigeon chicks peeping from building ledges, the day came when Sarah could hide her bulge no longer. She said she'd introduce her mother to her grandchild and Savage simultaneously, so that if her mother had to faint, it would just be the once.

The two took the subway, and passing over the Manhattan Bridge, they looked out at the tinsel skyline. He rubbed her belly.

The woman who answered the door looked young. Her hair was short and her brown eyes were constricted on the sight before her.

Sarah showed him in, her large belly leading.

Ms. Celeste Cooper locked herself in her room. Savage tended to the meal that had been cooking and Sarah set the table and then they watched television and were putting on their shoes to leave when her mother entered the room. She looked tired. She held a rosary.

"Ok," she said, "history repeats so why get riled up about it. Come here."

Savage limped over with one shoe on. She hugged him.

"Well," she said, "is it a boy or a girl?"

"We don't know," said Sarah.

Her mother closed her eyes. "You haven't been to a doctor." She pushed by Savage. "Look at me," she said to her daughter.

Then, "Girl," she pronounced.

"How do you know, mama?"

"Cause that baby's stealing your beauty. You ugly." She smiled. "And when will you two be getting married?"

"We won't," said Sarah.

Celeste's face darkened, and then Ms. Celeste Cooper locked herself in her room once again.

♤

He called his own parents a few days later. He'd been planning on doing what Sarah'd envisioned —waiting for the baby, then showing up with it and mother in tow—but with Sarah's mother knowing, he felt a scale had been tipped.

He called from a payphone on the corner.

"I'm going to be a father," he said.

He could hear his mother breathing. The sounds outside the booth: motorcycles, taxis, small birds. Finally, "I asked her to marry me," he said.

"When's the wedding."

"She said no."

"The devil," she said. "Who is she."

He looked past a crack in the booth's glass at Sarah standing there large bellied and waiting.

"She's beautiful," he said. "She's going to be an English professor."

Sarah smiled though she could not hear him.

"There's something else you're not telling me. I've known you since before you were born. Knew the grief you was going to give me—"

"Don't start, mama. Don't ruin—"

"Ruin what? Haven't heard from you in months. Don't understand your own life but here you are telling me you're ready to raise one from the dust. And you two got it so figured out you won't even do right by God. Meanwhile a year ago you were fighting with your sisters over a wishbone. Going to be a father. Hardly a man in feature but ready to assume the content."

He huddled over the receiver. She continued:

"Sprouting a sapling then leaving it to the weather."

"No, mama."

"Being a man is the weeding and the watering and the fertilizing. Doing it not just once but ten thousand times. Not just when the mood strikes but precisely when it doesn't. When there's nothing you'd rather less than change another diaper, warm another bottle. Nothing you'd rather than sleep cause you ain't since the baby arrived shrieking like a banshee—"

He dug in his pocket.

"—but still you must. Understand me, boy?"

"Yes ma'am," he said, looking at what he'd pulled out—two pennies, a wrapper. He cradled the phone to search his other pocket.

"That is a man. Who rises to feed, bathe, clothe, nurse, comfort, rock, and then work on the few winks he calls rest despite the urge to not just sleep but run. To run away gassed by the desires which in his weakest moments he calls manhood—promiscuity and debauchery and the like—conflating independence with irresponsibility and dancing with the devil till finally exhausted he crawls back tail tucked saying he's sorry, he confused lechery with manhood, and I say, No! That is not a man but a child with his toys. Bearded old and flabby but trapped within the confines of adolescence, a boy moved not by those higher callings—fatherhood, spirit—"

He dropped another quarter into the phone.

"—but by childish things not put away. Staying aslumber in the dream of his infancy."

"No, ma'am."

"No, ma'am," she said. "Speaks the part but inward's the fool."

"Yes, ma'am."

"Yes, ma'am," she mimicked. "Acts like he knows but does the opposite. Calls to say I will be a father and the mother studies English but won't marry me—and I still know you're conspiring. I've known you womb to adulterer and you cannot withhold from me."

He paused, and then he looked at Sarah. "She's black," he said.

The phone went silent. Then, "I don't think your father will appreciate this," she said and hung up.

♠

Sarah went into labor on a Sunday night but Savage was thinking about work. Lying beside her in the hospital room, pacing the hallway, stepping outside for the first cigarette of his life, not sleeping, waiting as the hours trickled into Monday morning and then afternoon when finally he stood in the waiting room calling his bar manager, cupping the receiver.

"I haven't slept since Saturday and the docs say she'll need a c-section but she won't—"

"I don't care if you have quadruplets. You get in here tomorrow and not one minute late because next thing you know you'll be calling out for a school play, telling me your son's the best tree you've ever seen."

"Jesus." Savage looked round the waiting room.

"Come in tomorrow or you're fired."

"John—" but he'd hung up.

And he remembered his daughter had been born on a Tuesday because he returned to work the next day but John had kept his promise.

♤

"That in the great tome of life there'll be an asterisk by my name explaining why, as my dad would say, I done what I done to who I done it to. I may have caused a wake of suffering behind me but I chose to do it with good reason." He quieted. Then he added: "Call it love."

He sat there quietly. The bartender put on music and a woman who'd been drinking alone bumbled out. A flash of sunlight. Then darkness. The smell of beer and wood. A slow Motown playing and I thought of Alfred. About how I'd come to expect his suicide and yet how it had struck me still. Maybe the harder for its inevitability. His ambivalence. How cold he'd been. How detached.

Savage took a long slug of beer and ordered another.

♠

The manager had told him not to show his face again and still closer to child than man, Savage had listened.

He went out to hunt work. Another jean jacket, jeans, a new pair of old boots, a toothpick he chewed on. He found work packing candles at a Jesus candle factory.

Months passed. One small job to another. Bussing tables, running errands, delivering groceries, loading trucks. Jobs that came and went with demand.

Returning home, he opened the door to their Harlem apartment. The books and the roaches and the tiny kitchen and their pull-out sofa. The cradle and the changing station and Sarah kissing him with Evelyn strapped to her full breast, Evelyn smelling of milk and shampoo. He took off his boots and she set out dinner. He sat on the window sill to a meal of rice, canned corn, beans. His months-old daughter squirmed on a blanket.

Sarah returned with a glass of water and

joined him. She was not happy. Had grown melancholic. He did his best to ignore her mood.

They ate.

"What is it?" she asked.

"Nothing," he said.

"Tell me."

He pushed his rolling tray away.

"One more year and you'll have graduated," he said.

"Baby." She reached for his hand. "I'll get a job after that."

He stood and looked down onto the street below. "All I'm doing is getting good at something there ain't no getting good at."

"I'm getting a degree for us."

"That diploma will have one name on it."

She stood and leaned her head on him. Evelyne cooed from the floor.

"Baby, if you want to go to school, I could work—"

"I wasn't made for school."

She let go of him and picked up Evelyne and patted her.

"A question for me just raises others and I'm left with more holes than when I begun." He looked at her. "You won't even marry me."

"Don't start." She picked up a pacifier.

"I'm a simple man."

She pushed it into Evelyne's mouth. "Man and wife," she said. "A wife just the oil to the man's ambition."

"I just want to make this right. To purify it."

"Is this dirty?" She gestured at their room.

He turned back to the window and grabbed the curtain. "Another year of this and we'll be talking two different languages."

"Baby," she said, rocking her daughter, but said nothing else.

He watched the cars passing below. "You'll be so smart you'll make me think my foot's my head and my arms—"

"Baby, stop it." She bounced their daughter.

"I never want to go back to school."

"What then."

He sighed. "I always thought I'd be great."

She smiled sadly. Her brown skin glistening. Evelyne the color of sun-dried wheat. The city sepiaed by twilight.

♤

Her sadness grew. Nights spent weeping. Days she would not eat. Her eyes turned dark, her moods more sullen. Months of this.

One day, he returned home to find Sarah crying, holding their shrieking naked baby over a sink of steaming water. The faucet running hot. The screaming. It's like he'd been waiting for this. Had been unconsciously planning.

She told him how Evey wouldn't eat, had cried most of the day, how the girl did not love her mother. She needed to clean her. To scrub her. Gently he took Evey away, eyeing that bath of scalding water, and then Sarah left for school.

He sat on the couch watching Evey sleep on the floor, the blanket rising and falling, her eyelids fluttering with the strange dreams of infancy.

A quadrangle of sun slowly crossed her and he was sitting there in a deep calculus when an image struck him: A man much the same only older. He worries about bills and money, about problems all domestic. He is alone, wifeless, daughterless. Horror crossed his face. A vision of a future that might be.

He got up and moved with absentminded purpose. He filled a bag with toys, baby clothes, formula, diapers. He filled another with things his own. The ring he'd proposed to Sarah with. He moved quickly.

He strapped his daughter to him and with bags slung he looked again at his home. Books stacked on the window sill. A pile of folded laundry.

He stepped into the cold hall and closed the door. Bundled and in solitary caravan, he headed out. Later, he found himself at the bank staring at an ATM screen. All the money they shared. Everything. It would only let him withdraw five hundred, but it would do, he thought.

II

♤

His bags occupy the empty bus seat beside him
until a large woman asks if it's taken. He shoves
his bags under his seat and the woman crams in
and he stares past his reflection at the night's
distancing city. Glimmering buildings. Soon both
father and daughter are asleep.

He awakes in darkness to her quiet crying. He
tries to feed her but she will not. Long highways
and oncoming headlights in a fine mist. He is hot
with her on his lap but there is nowhere else to
put her. He is sore.

"Ma'am," he nudges the woman beside him.

The woman smiles at Evey but then, sniffing,
she frowns.

He changes her as best he can in the bus'
bathroom and once more seated he is looking out
at sights previously reversed. Fields and
plantations rising beneath morning's glow.
Cornstalks piercing the fog. He remembers how
his father once said thirty days is not a month.

The window clouds with his breath and
someone snores. A conversation is carried in

whispers. What does he want. Nothing is enough. Evey cries but softly.

When they arrive to Elizabeth City, North Carolina, it is morning. He rents a car and buys a map and he is looking in the rearview at Evey in a car seat as they head south and then east into the rising sun. A bay glinting and a long bridge and he has time to think: Do we aim toward that which is already destined? He looks in the rearview and watches Evey awaken.

When they cross into the Outer Banks he opens his window to the ocean air. The radio plays and he's not felt so free since his first days in New York.

They come to Route 158. Outlets and furniture stores and beer marts and fast food and he turns into a parking lot.

From a payphone, he watches Evey through the car windshield. She's already crying.

The phone rings just once before a desperate voice answers.

"Hello?"

"Hi, baby."

Sarah whimpers. "Where are you?"

"I had to show her where I came from."

"I was throwing up all night," she said.

"I just need a week. Two. We'll fix things when I get back."

"Please. I'm sorry."

He looks at Evey. "Baby, I gotta go."

"No," she moans. "No, please … Come home."

"I will, baby," he says and hangs up.

♤

He drives them to the Wright Brothers Museum
and he pays the few dollars entry and he straps
Evey to his chest facing out. He paces marker to
marker explaining each and why he'd taken her
from her mother. She stares wide-eyed as they
climb Kill Devil Hill where a large monument
stands. A stone-etched quote he knows by heart.

From atop this dune he can see much of the
narrow island. Kites and small planes and the
ocean's tapestry broken by gleaming fins. The
smell of fish and sand and he covers Evey's head
with a small hat. The distant shouts of children.
He is standing there, looking, thinking, when
Evey begins to cry, then scream—inimitable and
wild—and he worries that there is no need met
that will curtail it. An outrage at existence.

He returns to the car with his daughter
screaming and he prepares lukewarm formula
and she will not drink. He sits in the car with the
door open, trying to feed her. People stare.

He puts her into her seat and he drives with
her crying. At a stoplight he looks in the

rearview: how much she resembles him.

He drives south, thirty minutes. More. Her crying is like a siren. He lumbers the car over a curb into an empty lot springing weeds through cracked asphalt.

He unbuckles her and checks her diapers. She will not eat. She will not stop crying. He grabs a blanket and he picks her up and feet sinking into the sand he climbs a path over wood-picketed dunes. The ocean opening like a kingdom, the crash of waves swallowing Evey's cries. Still holding her, he takes off his shoes and shirt and drops the blanket and pads over to the water. It is warm and in its green translucence he can see jellyfish, hundreds of thousands migrating on a warm current. They do not sting. They crowd as he wades ankle deep and he holds Evey's jogging feet in the water and she cries more. He wonders if she knows what he's done and if she could tell him why. He picks her back up and holding her head to his bare chest he bounces her and she begins to quiet. A pelican dives for small fish. A ship blows its horn.

♤

With a baseball cap pulled down he drives. Evey has taken her bottle. She has thrown up and he has cleaned her and they revisit the landmarks of his youth. She tosses her bottle to the car floor.

He parks across the street from a house and slumps into his seat. He watches the house. A one-story home on storm-weathered stilts. Its paneling yellowed to the color of sand. A seagull perched on its porch.

Something moves in a window and he sinks lower. Evey cries. He tries to hush her.

He angles his rearview that he can lay back and still watch the house. A car passes. He shuts his eyes.

When he awakens the car is hot and Evey is crying loudly. He turns to look and her face is red and slick and quickly he rolls down her window. He unbuttons her clothes and he thinks she needs water but all he's ever seen her drink is milk and formula and he knows nothing. What is he doing and why. He is reaching over his seat to take off her jumper when a knock comes at his window. It is a woman with dark hair and a small scar on her lip. His older sister Agnes.

"What are you doing here," she says, leaning in through his window.

He starts the engine.

"I just got off the phone with a woman named Sarah Cooper."

The engine does not start.

"She says you took her baby."

He tries the key again and the engine turns.

"I said you were in New York—"

He lurches the car and does not look back to see Agnes standing there holding her head. With every action he takes he knows more what he is about and he is afraid of himself.

He drives to a gas station. If Agnes has called the police they will find him. He sees someone leave their car running at a pump and he debates stealing that car. Then he looks back at Evelyne. "Shit," he says.

♤

He sits on a shaded bench outside of a deserted store. Between his legs an open bottle of water and his two bags. Evey sucks on his finger. His car is parked, hidden out of sight of the road, and the bench cannot be seen either. He has not seen any police. By the road stands a payphone.

He searches for a pacifier. Her bottles of formula are spoiling. He has not checked her diaper in some time.

The afternoon sun is brilliant and he squints despite the shade as he swaddles her. He will do what he should not in order to do what he must.

"Just give me two minutes," he says. He arranges her on the ground between his bags that she cannot roll over. She sucks on the pacifier fiercely. "Two minutes."

He runs to the payphone. One car passes and then another and their tires kick up dust. He puts the receiver to his shoulder and checks his pockets but they are empty. He curses.

He runs back and Evelyne is mewling. Her pacifier is in the gravel and he sucks it clean and dries it on his shirt. She needs some coaxing but she takes it.

Back at the phone with quarters, huffing, he dials.

"Hello?"

He silently reads the proclamation of love etched into the booth's glass, then, "Agnes. It's me," he says.

"You could've killed me!"

"Did you call the police."

"What?"

"Did you call the police."

He coils the phone's cord round his finger. His daughter's cries are like a baby gull's.

"Listen," he says, "I made a mistake. I'm heading back."

"To where."

"New York." He looks but can't see the bench.

"You better call me when you get there."

"Ok," he says.

She hangs up.

The sun greenhouses the phone booth and a police car rolls by and the cop driving it looks at him. Its lights and siren turn on. Then it screeches a u-turn and speeds away. Savage can hear his heart beating.

The sky is porcelain blue and the ocean roars dully.

He puts in another quarter and dials and it rings and then he hears Sarah's voice.

"Listen," he says, "we'll be back soon."

"You stole my daughter."

He looks back at the store. He can't hear

Evey.

"You took my baby!" she screams. "You kidnapped her!"

"She's my daughter. You can't—"

"Bring her back!"

"I will."

"Now!" she screams.

"Speak calmly, I—"

"I'm calling the police."

"Listen!" he shouts. "Listen," he says, but where do his words come from: "If you do you will never see her again."

Her begging is primal and horrid, but he hangs up.

He places another call.

When he returns to the bench he finds Evey face down in the ground. She is wailing as he wipes the dirt from her face and she is wailing as a taxi pulls up, its wheels grinding the pebbles beneath.

♤

They head back to Elizabeth City, off the island. If he had stayed, what might have been different. But from the barrel of the past we shoot our trajectories and Savage sits holding his sleeping daughter, staring out at shimmering water. The driver looks in his rearview.

They stop at the bus terminal. Savage counts out thirty two dollars and the driver turns to collect it. His face is red and his eyes bulbous and his arms burly.

"It ain't my business," he says, "but I never seen nobody hold a baby so awkward."

Savage thrusts him the money.

He stands in the bus terminal with his daughter strapped to him and a bag over each shoulder and he heads to the counter to enquire about the next bus to New York.

"Leaves in three hours," says the attendant. "Babies is free. Just one ticket then?"

Savage thanks him and is heading outside into the hot sun as the attendant calls after him, "So do you want that ticket? Sir?"

Outside, Savage watches friends wave to one another from passing cars. He stands and thinks. He's not eaten all day. What notions travel through his head.

He enters a diner and waiting to be seated puts down his bags and he takes out his wallet and counts his money. He wants a hamburger but with Evey still strapped to him he heads to the counter and orders a coffee instead. The waitress smiles.

"He's adorable," she says.

He does not correct her. "Thank you," he says, sitting at a stool, paying for his coffee.

Then, "Ma'am," he calls, reaching into his bag, "could you warm this." He takes out a bottle.

"Sure, hon." She takes it and disappears into the kitchen, but when she returns it is with a coffee, the bottle, and a sandwich. "This was going to the trash."

His eyes well. "I'll pay for it, ma'am"

She waves him off.

He tests the milk on his wrist but it is hot so he waits. All there is to read is the menu so he does. Then Evey begins to cry. Her eyes not newborn gray but brown. Her frown could break a heart. He stares at his untouched sandwich and his stomach grumbles and he rocks her and whispers, "Hush, little one. Hush."

♤

He is full and tired but he has nowhere to go. He walks around that quaint city, his shoulders slick with sweat under his bags.

The day is dulling behind a cloud when he comes to a bed and breakfast. Its sign sways from no breeze he can feel and its curtains are sun-bleached. A bell rings his entrance and at the front desk is a man of indeterminate age.

"Yes, sir," says the man, putting down a newspaper.

"How much for a night."

The man looks at Evelyne.

"Just the two of you?"

Savage nods.

The man looks at the baby and then at Savage and then at the cuckoo clock on the wall.

"Forty eight."

He cannot afford it but he takes out his wallet anyway. To count what he already knows.

"Ok," says Savage.

The man reaches for a ledger and a key and he puts on glasses.

"I'll give you a discount," he says, opening the book. "We just need some ID."

Savage stops. His ID peeks from a fold.

"I lost it," he says.

The man looks up from where he's marked with a finger. "We need something," he says.

"Yes, sir," says Savage, replacing his wallet. "Well, thank you anyway."

The man looks again at the clock. He props his glasses on his head and rubs his eyes.

"Listen, friend," he says, "perhaps you've hit upon hard times."

"I'll be fine," says Savage. "Thank you." He turns.

"My aunt has a spare room," exclaims the man. "Cheap but none of the amenities. I wouldn't normally but, well … My wife takes over in an hour. She gets here and I'll walk you over. Go ahead and sit in that chair there. You can sleep if you like. I'll get you some water."

Savage looks at him.

"Don't fret," says the man, stepping out of the room. "We gotta take care of our own."

♤

They walk through the town, Savage a few paces behind and carrying Evey and his bags for he's refused any help. The man has a limp and he hobbles down the street nodding to passersby.

Downtown gives onto suburbs and soon the man turns and calls out, "Stop walking so far back. Legs are for hurryin'."

Savage catches up and the man insists on taking a bag and they pass beneath low hanging trees and the evening brings respite from the heat.

"So what's your name."

Savage lies.

"Good to meet you." He looks at Evey sleeping, drooling onto Savage's shoulder. He seems to dismiss a thought. He kicks a stone.

They walk in silence. The man spits.

"Name's Joe," he says. "South Carolina born and raised."

Their feet crunch a pebbly road.

"Well." But the man says nothing else, his face darkened by the shadow of his brow. They climb a hill and the lights of the town twinkle under an orange sky.

"We'll come to her house shortly," he says. "Everyone calls her Bonnie. Old as roads."

They walk on and then with no introduction the man says: "Try anything with her and I'll murder you," but unsatisfied, he adds: "I'm a man of means and methods and I'll hunt you down."

Their shadows cast long behind them as they keep on and Savage ducks beneath branches. The ground turns from gravel to dirt. They swat at mosquitoes.

"That's the house up yonder."

Savage looks up the road. Through a thicket, the moss of a roof. They push aside brambles and it is getting dark as they near. A house low and damp. Shuttered windows. Rotting wood. Joe bangs on the screen's frame.

"What," comes a voice.

"It's me. Joe."

Footsteps approach from within. The door opens onto a silhouette.

"What."

A lamp clicks on and a short, old woman appears. Constellations of warts, a soiled dress.

"I brought you a guest," says Joe.

"Another one?" She wipes her hands in a dirty apron.

Joe clears his throat, introduces Savage.

"How long's he staying?"

"A few days."

"Can't he speak."

"Yes, ma'am," says Savage.

"Well, what is that." She points a gnarled finger, stabbing the screen separating them.

"My daughter."

"Lord. Babies is extra. Where's the mother."

The two look at Savage.

"Dead," he says.

"Good," she pronounces. "Cause I'll have no lechery. Don't care if you're married or not. It's the way of the devil. Nothing but trouble it brings and if you don't believe me just look at what you got." She begins to shut the door and then she speaks through a crack. "Five a night and fifty cents for the child. Food is extra."

"Yes, ma'am."

She shuts it.

They stand there silently. Then Joe bangs the door again. "Auntie!" he shouts.

"What!" she yells, ambling from around the house's corner. "Lord."

Joe drops the bag he'd been carrying. "Well, you need anything you give me a call."

"You know I ain't got no phone," she says.

The man waves goodbye as he disappears into the forest, leaves rustling and insects chirping and the last tweets of birds.

Bonnie turns and heads back the way she came.

"Well," she shouts, "you coming?"

He picks up the other bag and follows her, making his way through knee-high weeds until he comes to the door she is unlocking.

♤

The room is small and glows by a single lamp. It is humid and decorated with a deer head and an old unidentifiable painting. It smells of mothballs and smoke but it is clean and has a sink and a window. A small bed sits in the corner and the carpet is threadbare but Savage has never known luxury. Bonnie lumbers back outside.

He drops his bags and looks down at Evey sleeping against him. Another door stands opposite the entrance but it is locked. He guesses it opens onto the house for he can hear the old woman behind it.

She returns hefting a metal basinet. Rusted and squeaky.

"Thank you, ma'am," he says.

"I ain't doin' you no favors," she says, unpacking a bag of yellowed quilting from beneath the room's bed and then taking a pouch from her apron.

"How many nights."

He does not think. "One week."

"Six nights then." She counts on her fingers. "Thirty. Plus the baby …" She closes her eyes. Her lips move. "Thirty two fifty."

He takes out his wallet and hands her bills. She folds them into her pouch and counts out fifty cents change.

"What about food," he says.

"Seventy five cents a day. Breakfast and supper." Her eyes fall onto his charge. "I ain't got nothin' for that."

He gives her more money.

"I lock the door at nine. Come in after that and you're sleeping in the woods." She stares at him. Eyes like youth's embers. "I'll be back directly," she says and turns to go.

"I'll need a pot and a hot plate for her milk," he calls.

She stops. "That'll be extra," she says.

♠

He has pulled the basinet close to the bed and changed and fed Evelyne and watched her sleep and then had a fitful rest of his own. By twilight he is sleeping like a man entombed. He awakens to a cold breakfast on a tray beside him and Evey is crying once more. Her tiny limbs flailing and the basinet squeaking and he picks her up, bobs her, but she will not stop.

He boils water and prepares formula and there is little left. His money will not last much longer and once depleted he'll have to return home. Why has he left Sarah. She was depressed. He'd once overhead her say to Evey: "I know I'm supposed to love you." Then there was the scalding water and that Sarah would not marry him. But suckling his daughter he wonders: Was this the greatness he'd dreamed of? Or had he settled for much less? No schooling, no kindness or compassion, only that universal ability to destroy. He sits on the bed feeding his daughter and begins to weep. Then he smells her, remembers his own needs. He looks around for a bathroom but there is none.

Pushing aside the tray—cold toast and cold oats and cold coffee—he straps Evey to his chest and heads outside. The sun ascends over a forest mad with bugs and birds. Lush and opaque. Yet he prefers a toilet and so he is nearing the house's front door when he sees a trampled path. At its end is an outhouse. He sighs. Holding his daughter, he approaches it. He opens its door and flies ambush him. Hundreds of moths on its walls like fuzzy drapes. He walks back to his room and takes the hand towel from the sink and shutting the screen door behind him returns to the outhouse. He flaps the towel at the moths and they scatter round him in a living whirlwind.

With Evey pressed to him, he sits there in the stench.

♠

Repeating Aunt Bonnie's directions aloud, he finds his way back onto gravel, then macadam, and soon he is back in that quiet town. The sun is scathing.

He finds a payphone and places a call but no answer. The phone returns his coin and he tries again. Nothing. He wanders the downtown and soon he knows it well and he heads to a park with a few books he found on a curb.

Cradling Evey, he sits on a bench and tries one book and then another. If anyone asks he's on unemployment and her mother is dead. He sits pretending to read as the sun inches toward the horizon, until he thinks he hears Evey say mama.

He calls again.

♤

Days spent wandering and sitting in a small library. One who's never read trying to find what will move him, biding time breakfast to supper. Then one day he calls from the payphone and an answering machine picks up. If it's you, leave a message. Please. He does not.

He reads in the library and it bores him to no end but he cannot stay outside for he'll draw attention. Sometimes he just sits marveling at his daughter, calm as long as she's swaddled. She seems heavier now and when back in their room she rolls over and it seems a miracle. He is overjoyed and then he is overcome. Why doesn't she pick up, he thinks, shifting the blame. What mental leaps.

On his fifth day the heat is at a record high but he is chilly with sweat in the air-conditioned library. The librarian, her hair freshly curled, welcomes him with a book and a pastry. He knows he's overstayed.

He declines both.

"I never see you eat," she smiles.

He saunters to his regular chair and table where she has already stacked his books. He frowns and sits and pretends to read, lost in thought.

He leaves his book open and grabs the changing bag he carries and with Evey on his back he heads into the weighty heat, the white sky blinding. His boots clop his way to the payphone. He puts in a quarter and dials and waits and is about to hang up when a voice answers.

"Hello?"

She is weak and distant.

"It's me," he says.

She begins to cry.

He is silent.

"Please come home. I'll do whatever you want," she says.

He hears a drumming. He pulls the headset from his ear and the drumming turns to slapping. Outside it rains. The stone shingles of a church darken.

He crosses himself.

"I thought you might kill her," he says.

The rain pummels. Thunder booms. Then, "I'm calling the police," she says quietly.

♤

He slugged his beer. The bartender went off to serve a customer, and I thought again of Alfred. Friend, teacher, writer. Placed so much onus on every word that none was ever good enough. Could make you bleed with envy at his stories but could drive himself mad over a sentence. The price he paid. I missed him dearly.

I cleared my throat.

"My friend Alfred St. Mary hoped reincarnation was real so he could try again."

Savage's eyes narrowed, felined.

"Jesus," he said, "I'm here bequeathing you my life and you're daydreaming. Here I am saying Dear God look what I've done—a fury of a life, a blind shot at greatness if only by the bravado of my existence—and you're interrupting the tale." He clenched the bar. "Should I worry about the writer I've chosen."

"No," I said.

"No." He looked off, turned back. "Then how dare you interrupt me."

We sat there, a resentment bubbling.

"What," he said.

I shook my head.

"What," he said again, agitated.

"It's fiction. Your story."

He sat there quietly. Then he laughed, loud and hard and without humor.

"You're drunk," he said. He drank more. "A woman tells you she was kidnapped as a baby. That she remembers the calluses of her kidnapper's fingers. The timbre of his voice. The beat of his heart. Tells you she can remember his words." He looked at me. "Do you dismiss her story as fantasy."

I did not answer.

"Is it possible that her memory spans all the way to birth."

He waited.

"You cannot dismiss it." He huffed. "When she tells you she remembers the sourness of her kidnapper's breath, it's not the scent she remembers nor the fray of his shirt but the smell and strain of their relationship. And if in her autobiography she remembers shoes or a house that did not exist, it does not matter for we must lend credence to the feelings elicited for those are the truth. And so if my story has acquired impossible frills or the diction of my retelling does not jibe with the record of history, so be it, it does not matter, for all I've done is articulate what was thought and present then, even if the sky was cloudy when I called it clear." He closed his eyes as though reciting: "For the heart knows what the mouth intends."

THE FATHER

♤

He lets the phone drop and it hangs there pendulating. Evey sleeps as a raw arithmetic enters his mind. It will not take them long to find him. The rain has abated and the sun's returned and he must be gone before the ground dries— less time than that.

He steps out of the booth and with Evey thumping on his back he hurries toward his rented room. A man and baby galloping through the streets, iterated in storefront windows. He must slow. He does.

His heart beats quickly and he is sweating. Evey's eyes are wide apertures devoid of abstraction, reason, purpose, portals of little discernment. Suddenly he stops. He curses himself for having left a bag at Bonnie's. He'd known to be a man who carried his home. He'll lose clothes and laundry soap and a towel and a blanket and whatever else. He has his knife, a sweater, his money—at least he has that. He'll have to leave the rest. But you go to God naked or not at all. So be it, he thinks. I'm that much closer.

He heads toward the bus station. He has an inkling that the police will move quickly. Vague notions of how things work. They'll be looking for a man with a baby. He's ditched one car already and won't be able to rent another. He hurries.

They'll put word out: the bus station, the train station. He thinks about turning himself in, but the courts would side with the mother, and even if he's not jailed, he does not know what Sarah's capable of. Perhaps this is the greatness he'd dreamt of: a private one.

He turns the corner and seeing a sheriff's cruiser becomes self conscious of his gait. His step, the swing of his arms. I'm just a man walking with his daughter, he thinks.

The cruiser slows and he can feel the sheriff's sunglassed eyes following him but he walks on until it passes and he turns a corner.

"Watch where you're going," says a man carrying groceries.

Soon he's at the bus station. A small, empty terminal. No one at the window. He spots a bathroom and prays it vacant and it is. Small, spartan, clean. He locks the door and drops his bag and Evey gurgles and he thinks. He crouches and unzips the bag. Diapers, baby clothes, powder, wipes, only three bottles and two are empty. He looks into the key-scratched, full-length mirror and does not recognize his reflection.

He accommodates his bag's contents and

tosses a few invaluable diapers to make a hollow
within. He unstraps Evey and must toss more to
fit her carrier and then he swaddles her. Eyes big
as prey. He tries to give her a pacifier but she will
not take it. "Please," he begs. Her tiny lips resist.
He picks her up and rocks her and whispers and
her contorted face relaxes and he tries her
pacifier again. She takes it. A knock comes at the
door.

"One moment," he says.

He flushes the toilet.

He thinks that if this weren't meant to be
then God would intervene. The police would
burst in. Evey would scream. He runs the sink
and then the hand dryer and he looks down at
her tiny body and her eyes of unbound trust.
How he adores her. He zips the bag that he can
still see her glaring eyes. "Just give me two
minutes," he says.

He carefully shoulders the bag and tests its
weight: it will hold. Through its opening he
inserts his hand that he is caressing her as he
unlocks the door to confront the officer waiting
there but it is just a woman holding her child.

"Pardon me," she says rushing past.

He looks down at Evey's large eyes. If God did
not want this ...

Departures flap on the board above and
Washington D.C. flips to Raleigh. He rings a bell
at the ticket window and a stoic, gray-haired
man appears.

"Did the bus to D.C. leave yet," asks Savage.

"Leaving now," says the man.

Savage looks out the window. A driver loads bags.

"One," he says.

The man looks at him and then he pushes buttons and a ticket prints.

"Thirteen fifty," he says. "Better hurry."

Savage feels the pacifier fall. He looks down and through the aperture can see her gearing to cry and without thinking stuffs his grimy finger into her mouth. With his other hand he scrambles for his money and he places it on the counter and grabs the ticket.

He runs outside toward the bus. "Wait!" he yells, standing before its closed door. Its engine has already started.

The driver shakes his head. But then the door opens with a wheeze. "Get on," he says.

Savage lurches through the aisle as Evey lets out a single cry. A man looks at him curiously.

♤

He can't help but feel it a dream. Nightmare or lucid or both. He takes his daughter from his bag and gives her the pacifier and cradles her looking up with wonder. Her bronze skin strikes him. He looks out the window. Cars and trucks and light poles and he falls asleep and when he awakes Evey is crying—her pacifier on the floor and she tilting precariously off his lap. He grabs her. How easy it is to do what can never be undone. How tired he is.

They arrive to Washington D.C. and he follows a dome until the Capitol rises before him. The sun is angling and a cool breeze scatters old tree blossoms. He is here. A man of signs, omens, and instincts. His arrival is fate's approval.

With his bag over his back and his daughter strapped to his stomach, he looks up at the Capitol's white dome. "You will not remember," he says, "but it is for you that we have come." He looks down at her. "Hurry up and grow."

His boots tack on the sidewalk. He washed

from a sink this morning, but when was the last time he showered or laundered. Like a creature at home in cardboard. Still, a group of tourists ask him to take their picture and he does.

♤

He walks. Tall, proud monuments give onto row houses. He peers into dust-shelved stores and rundown bodegas. Shuttered shops. Men on stoops. Eviction notices. The drug-addled. The afternoon is bright and provides sad contrast to his predicament. He'd prefer this morning's rain. Or a tempest. He sits down on a bench but his grumbling stomach forces him on and he walks a few blocks until he comes to a diner whose windows have taped-over bullet holes. The rusty door cranks his entrance and he sits at a stool. A man eats a meager sandwich.

A waitress approaches.

"What can I get you," she asks, mouth bright with lipstick.

A chalkboard lists a few items.

"A coffee," he says.

"That it?"

He reads the board. "And toast."

She walks off.

He opens his bag and shakes a can of formula. Little left. He looks round. Walls stained and browned and the floor tacky and the tables dirty. The shattered window casts a web shadow.

The waitress returns with coffee thick as syrup and a dry piece of toast.

"Dollar twenty five," says the woman.

He pulls out his wallet and takes out two dollars and then he gives her his last one too.

"Just two," she says.

"That's for you," he says.

She narrows her eyes and tucks the dollar into her apron.

He wants to tell her that he needs work and shelter and that he is lost. That he knows no one and that he cannot return from whence he came but he says nothing.

"You're not from around here," she says.

"Just going for a walk."

She shakes her head. Her large hair is a wig. "Dangerous place to walk if you ain't got business being here."

He bites his toast. It crunches. "There's no place I have business being."

"Where you from," she says.

"North Carolina."

She nods. "Then you ought to know better."

She heads off and returns with plated butter. She looks at Evey and bites her lip and then she heads to the register to continue the receipt tallying he'd interrupted. He eats and drinks slowly until finally he musters the courage to ask if she'll fill a bottle with warm milk. Thus emboldened, he asks if she can sterilize some bottles too.

"In boiling water," he says, handing her the

empty ones.

"Like I don't know," she grunts, taking them. "Look at me. How many do you think have sucked life from these?" She grabs herself. Then, "Seven," she says. "Enough to know no baby can survive on cow milk."

"Nor can a man survive on coffee," he says, sipping his.

"Well," and is heading off when she turns back, "a baby needs a mother. Even a good-for-nothing one." She goes off into the small kitchen.

He stands outside, holding his sated, sleeping child, regretting. He is afraid. He has placed their lives in fate's hands but with hesitation at his vow. That he'll not return. That he'll raise his daughter not to take root in the bourgeois but in turmoil, in life's oil pan. He enters the diner again.

"Miss," he says.

The waitress looks up from her receipts.

"I was too ashamed to let on what you probably guessed, but the mother of my child is dead and we are homeless and I need work and a room and I will do anything."

She scratches her head beneath her hair. Skin the color of rust. Lipstick on her teeth. She heads off into the kitchen. The man who'd been watching the exchange returns to his sandwich. After some time, the waitress waddles back out through a swinging door.

"We need a dishwasher," she says. "Come after the lunch rush."

♤

He spends the night in the diner's basement. A cot and a small cushioned box for a crib and no windows. Boxes and crates and a single lightbulb whose switch he'll have to turn off from the top of the stairs and return down in darkness. The basement smells of grease and he can hear the pitter-patter of mice but there is a bathroom upstairs and they've given him a towel and he is grateful.

♤

He keeps Evey in her makeshift crib in an alcove
and he washes dishes with her strapped to his
back. Scraping a pan or drying the endless plastic
cups, he remembers Sarah's smile or some
kindness. He could go back, but more days pass.
Weeks turn to months. Evelyne grows.

The chef is the owner and the waitress Mary
his sister and once a week they pay him. He buys
thrift-shop clothes for Evey and dresses her as a
boy and cuts his own hair close to the scalp. He
eats hamburgers and eggs and he grows too, his
body filling what he'd years ago claimed: man.

No trees mark the changing of the seasons,
just concrete forms slowly crumbling. The air
cooling. Certain thoughts fortifying as others
dissipate.

He talks to Evey. She's so heavy that by day's
end he's sore, and he is washing a stack of plates
when he starts to tell her of the mother who'd
with time grown more depressed until the day he
came home to find her crying that her child did
not love her. Pulling at her own hair and

weeping.

"What do you say to that," he says over his shoulder as he scrubs. "What can you say but, Of course she loves you. And your mother cried: Then why won't she eat? She'd rather starve than take my milk. And she wept like a madwoman, like someone losing the container to her insides."

He builds the mythology of his daughter's creation, that swamp from which heroes spring, and at night, when it is just the two of them, he reads to her. Books he struggles with himself but that read in his drawl mesmerize her. He cannot help but think that he is forging himself, though for what.

♠

Mary corners him one day as he's heading upstairs carrying a large box of napkins. Evey's strapped to his back.

"Yes, ma'am," he says.

"It's been almost four months."

"Yes, ma'am."

"We've paid, housed, and fed you, and you've done all we asked."

"Yes, ma'am."

"We've paid in cash." She stands arms akimbo. "And we've maintained our silence. But one starts to ask questions."

They stand in the alcove's light. Beside them the cardboard crib his daughter's outgrown.

"Where you came from and what happened to her mother and how you'll work without question of pay, even if it's little predictable one week to the next. But you don't complain and I feel as though you'd work for nothing. And my heart sinks."

She sighs.

"A man on the run. The sins we run from

return tenfold and woe unto us should we let you to stay.

"But tomorrow is Christmas," she continues, "and we plan on having you for dinner. You're not family but you got none to turn to and no one should be alone on the day of our Lord. But after that, you have two weeks. It's not that you haven't done a fine job, but stay any longer and I will have to know what I'm sure we'd both rather I not." She stops him from speaking. "No need to add sin to the lies already told. Just accept our invitation and begin to make your arrangements."

"Yes, ma'am."

"I have someone who might be able to help you. But after you leave it's best we not speak again."

Her lips purse.

"Now, put down the napkins," she says. "And let's pray. Tomorrow the Lord comes."

♤

The card in his wallet says he is Vincent Laguria and now Savage works in a supermarket bagging groceries while Evey stays with his super's wife— with three children of her own—that when Savage proposed daycare, Harietta said, "Sure. She'll just suck the other tit."

He has wanted to but he has not called. Cannot risk it. A half year gone.

He is bagging groceries on a Sunday when a woman steps up to the register. Seated in her cart is a child Evey's age. The cashier rings up the woman's groceries and, reaching into her purse, the woman bends to kiss her daughter. Savage is suddenly struck by a vision. He thinks he should return. But brought on by the unexpected, these moments fade just as quickly. They leave their accumulating residue but he learns to wait out the guilt.

He vaguely smiles and places the paper bags into the cart and watches them go.

♤

They live hand to mouth in a tiny apartment. He thinks that no man or woman should raise a child alone, and he lies in the dimming light on his squeaking bed imagining if the roles had been reversed. If after a life's absence, Evey one day knocked on his door and said, "Dad." He looks at her playing on the floor and starts to tear up from the horror.

He stands and turns the light on and mashes peas on the small table serving as their kitchen counter. To return now would be to go to the shackle.

She calls to him and he brings her peas and a sippy cup of water and all around them are books. The judge would side with the mother. With the irrecoverable tears of lost time. But Your Honor, I saw the skewed look in her eyes. The glint of terror. There are instincts concealed within us that setting and circumstance ripen—love, revenge, murder, salvation, redemption, fear—and both of our darkest were instigated. Perhaps more of a man would've sought help. Or maybe my daughter'd be dead, shuffled off by some gruesome news I didn't want to imagine then or now. Judge, I tell you that afraid for the life of your child—with no money or support but a mother's gnarling hands—coming home with the looping imagery of the horror you read in the morning paper, you'd've done the same. What separates us is not the deed but the robe and the upbringing. Yet replace yours with mine and we'd be reversed. You begging and me judging. So look on me, your Honor, as though into a mirror.

"Papa," she calls to him as he faces their sole window, view unto a brick wall. "Wawa," she calls in a voice her mother's never heard and never will.

"Yes, baby," he says, looking at her covered in mashed peas, picking up the empty cup from where she'd tossed it, and then standing again in contemplation, justifying acts done and those yet not.

♠

Evey is asleep in her cradle and he writes by nightlight. He fills pages with explanation and consolation though none's to be had. Shadows dance across his page. A siren passes by outside.

He starts again: Dear Sarah ... but he is not satisfied.

He wears two sweaters and the radiator kicks and hisses. He hears the gentle breathing of his daughter and begins to cry. Tears leaving florets of ink but he cannot stop. He shifts in his chair, his only furniture but a cradle and a dresser he uses as desk and table. Pangs of fear and lust and love. He cannot stop crying. He writes pages. He spouts illusions and begs forgiveness and absolution. That he will endure the anger she bears and return her daughter so long as he can still be a father. All he wanted was to protect her but his life's been the juggle of hidden gods. How is this greatness. He writes of loneliness, despair, paranoia. Perhaps now the FBI is involved and he cannot live like this. He bangs the dresser and Evey stirs yet he does not move until the peals dissipate and he looks at what he's written. He crumples the pages and begins anew. Sarah, he writes. Your daughter's well. Me.

♤

Evey holds his finger. Bumbling forward, bundled in used, mismatched clothes. So too is he dressed. Wool cap, scarf, sweatshirt, jacket, and boots.

Their breaths balloon. "Wawa!" she shouts, pointing up.

"Snow," he says. In his pocket is the enveloped letter.

They stop in a convenience store and enter a photo booth and a light flashes and then they wait.

He walks her down an aisle and uses a pair of scissors to cut himself from the photo just produced and then he places what remains into the envelope.

They head to the bus station. Large, bustling, high-ceilinged. He looks up at the board and he chooses the farthest destination from which they can return the same day. Holding Evey's hand as she tries to pull off her scarf, he heads to a ticket counter.

"Round trip to Pittsburgh."

"When're you leaving," says the teller, small eyes set in a large head.

"On the next one."

"Returning when."

"Is there a return today."

"Every two hours."

"Four then."

The man furrows his large brow. "That's a seven hour drive each way."

"Have to say hello to someone."

"Phones exist," says the man.

♤

It is no small feat to travel with a small child, but Evey has grown used to small quarters and odd circumstance. She amuses herself with the stuffed dog her mother once gave her and he reads to her and feeds her jelly sandwiches and curled marsupial she falls asleep on the empty seat beside him. Later she will awaken and climb on his lap and kissing her soft head he will look out the window and she will point at things all of the same name.

When they arrive it is mid-afternoon and the sky is white and it is cold. His limbs ache and he is hungry but because of traffic they have little time. Carrying Evey, he jaunts down streets until he finds a mailbox and though he's traveled seven hours to do just this he hesitates.

He hands the letter to his daughter.

"Drop it in," he says, opening the box.

"Uh oh," she says as it disappears.

"Yes, uh oh," he repeats and jogs them back to arrive just as the bus doors close. The bus is mostly empty and Evey races up and down the aisle, pawn to her father's whim.

♤

Later he will think on all the things that had to be just so. But that morning, there is only an odd presentiment.

He leaves Evey with Harietta, the super's wife. She pats the child's bottom into her apartment and Savage heads off to work.

His manager fawned over his southern ways and he is a cashier now. He's on break, chatting with a coworker named Rebecca who fixes her hair as she speaks. Opening his bag, he realizes he forgot his lunch.

Out in spring's warmth, passing a bar's open door, he sees a television playing and stops. It's him. Curlier hair and thinner face. His senior high school portrait. He angles himself to watch without being seen. The local news, a kidnapping, the photo he'd taken with Evey months ago. And then it's her, Sarah. He's too far to hear but straining his eyes he can just read the lagged captioning: Bring her home. It cuts to the reporter and then to advertisement and then she's gone. He's lightheaded. Wonders if he saw what he saw but he knows it was real.

The sun gleams off storefronts and cars. He is sweating. He hurries past the deli to which he'd been heading and turns at a corner and then another and heads back from where he came, panicking. He looks over his shoulder. No plan but to leave. To uproot. He jumps into a store and buys sunglasses and electric clippers and a cap. Then he heads back to the supermarket and stands in its entrance looking to see if they're talking about him. He does not think they are. He enters.

"You're back early," says Rebecca, smiling, dimpled.

"I forgot my backpack," he says, reaching under the register.

"You look like you saw a ghost."

"Tell Janice I'm sick," he says and then he leans in to whisper, "When do you get off."

She blushes. "Five."

"You still have your car."

She nods.

"I'll meet you here."

He looks at her and she nods again.

It is a long walk to his apartment but he needs time to think. He makes eye contact with none. Vague plans clarify and he knows he must hurry.

Soon he's at his building. Dilapidated and squat. He bangs on the front door and can hear children laughing. Harietta answers.

"Harry," he says, "I gotta take Evey."

"Why're you back so early?"

"My father's sick," he says. "We need to see him. We'll be gone a few days."

"They ain't eaten yet," she says. Pandemonium behind her at which they both turn to look. "Take in your kid and suddenly the whole neighborhood's dropping off their children. Bunch of wild monkeys. Look at this," she tugs on her red-streaked dress. "One of 'em got into my makeup." She sighs and steps aside. "Well, go ahead."

He enters a dark apartment. Children running, shouting. Tables covered with papers and play-dough and fingerpaints and he finds Evey alone in a corner, pretending to read. She looks up and squeals.

♠

He has his daughter and two packed bags and is waiting outside of the grocery store. His hope is to leave before the evening news. When Rebecca exits, she is perfumed and made up.

"This is Evelyne." He stretches out Evey's hand.

Rebecca's smile betrays surprise as she takes it.

Evey retracts and huddles into her father and they stand there getting colder with the sun's descent, shadows in lank puppetry.

"I need a favor." He clears his throat.

Rebecca blows into her hands.

"We don't know each other well," he says.

"What do you need," she says.

He is holding his bags and child and his load is heavy. He looks down at the sidewalk. Remnants of a long dead pigeon. People enter the store behind them.

"I need to go far," he says.

"I'll take you," she replies.

♤

They drive in a beat-up car and Evey is asleep in the back cordoned by their bags. A twilit highway. Golden guardrails. Savage deep in thought for before they left he called her. Sarah. He sits there little warmed by wheezing vents, wondering why he did it, why he'd tensed the manhunt, yet there he'd stood in a phone booth, debating whether to hang up when she answered.

"Hello?" she said, "Hello?" perhaps already guessing it him. "Is it you?"

He was silent. By what strange and sadistic impulse was he moved. Or was it longing. Perhaps he was populated by two within.

"Come home." The word sticking like a pike.

She kept on. Told him that she wouldn't press charges, that she just wanted her daughter. To see him. To sit on the sill, laughing and plotting, and why had he done it. "Speak to me." But he did not, knowing the impossibility of her promises.

He watches headlights approach and disappear and he feels that much like himself she too is bifurcated, one mind promising what the other cannot give.

♤

I sat there wondering how he'd made me complicit and to what end. He must have known, telling his story to a stranger, what he risked. Maybe this was what he counted on. That once his life had been recorded, the onus of justice would rest with another.

"What," he said.

I shrugged.

"You're wondering how I could it."

I sat silently and then, "Yes," I said, looking at my tumbler holding nothing but a meniscus of water.

His gaze was physical, pressing.

"Well," he said, "is it better to have a vile parent or none at all. To know only a doting father or to be at the mercy of the faucet of your mother's conditional love, shut at the slightest provocation. If Evey didn't eat, it was because she hated her mother. If she cried, the same. If she dirtied her diapers right after she'd been changed, it was out of spite. That's how it went. A fickle love and a fickle self worth and there's no telling what she might have done. And it's easy to sit here now and judge what seems a decision made but I don't feel there ever was one. I saw before me the fate of my daughter in the hands of a woman slowly unraveling. That was what I realized during that phone call. That there was nothing Sarah could say to reverse the stitch of our lives. I could only move forward."

♤

They drive in silence. Rebecca looking at the road and he out his window and the child quiet in the back. He has given little explanation and as lampposts clock the night he feels he owes her.

"Thank you," he says.

"You're welcome," she says.

They drive on. A quiet rent by the car's rattles and a staticky radio.

"You will hear things," he says, "but I want you to know that I always acted in my daughter's best interest."

She nods, her knuckles white on the steering wheel for the cold.

"You don't need a map," he says.

She shakes her head. "I used to do this drive all the time. An ex-boyfriend."

When he awakens he sees a skyline twinkling past the wires of a suspension bridge.

"I'm sorry," he says. "I didn't realize I was so tired."

"It's ok. She's awake." She glances at the

rearview.

He turns to look and Evey sits between bags, huddled under blankets, her eyes wide. She babbles.

"I have to change her," he says.

They pull off at a gas station and he wipes and changes her and watches Rebecca fill the tank. He has thrown off the hunt with a phone call, but he has no plan, little money, and no shelter or work. At least the struggle might soon be over. He looks up again and Rebecca is watching him through the glass. He'll soon have to ask her the impossible.

Munching chips and peanuts, they drive. The city blinking its morse in the distance, the car thumping across another bridge.

"You should spend the night," he says. "It's late."

"I was planning on it. There's a cheap place I know."

She turns them off the highway, her glasses reflecting neon lights. Rowhouses and liquor stores. Bodegas, graffiti, police cruisers. A neighborhood darkened by its broken lampposts. Caterwauling through a car window that won't close.

They pull up to a small motel and Savage looks up at its sign glowing only three letters. "Let's put it under your name."

"Ok," she says.

Carrying his bags and Evey crying from hunger and fatigue, he follows Rebecca in. A plastic plant the fluorescent lobby's only adornment. A manager who looks like he's not slept in days. Savage puts down his bags to get his wallet. Just twenty dollars a night but he can only afford one.

♤

The bed smells of cigarettes. The towels of
bleach. The room's bright from the motel sign
and he shuts the curtains but they're translucent.

Rebecca showers and he feeds Evey a mashed
banana and chips. She chews them with her new
teeth. She demands more and waddles after him
and then she tries to help as he accommodates
pillows to form a bed on the floor. No worse than
she's slept in before.

They lie on the floor and he's reading her a
book when Rebecca emerges from the bathroom.
Steam billows in. Long, wet hair. They look at
one another and trade places and he is thankful
for the shower.

Bands of light from passing cars meter the
ceiling and the room glows red from an alarm
clock. The two of them lie facing opposite walls.
No laughter or alcohol to instigate what's
expected. A punch line they don't know how to
arrive at.

She's dressed in a t-shirt and underwear and

he the same and he can smell the soap from her skin. He can hear Evey's soft snoring.

He can feel Rebecca roll over but he does not turn. To couple not from passion but obligation. If he angles his head just so, he can see his daughter. He tries to summon courage when suddenly Rebecca is licking his neck. Clothes are shed. Her pale, thin frame grinding his muscular figure, sheets nested round them, the cheap mattress caving to her muffled moans and quickening its spring. Its precedent he can't remember. Her nails are digging into his chest and her jaw slackening when luminous eyes appear by the bed's foot.

"Papa?"

Rebecca's sprawled across him and Evey's asleep and he wakes up in a panic. He is sweating and hot and has been dreaming but remembers only the feeling. He needs water. On the ceiling is a crack or a spider he can't tell. Then it moves.

He slowly peels away Rebecca's arm and he is trying to squirm out from beneath her when she awakens. Naked. Smiling.

"I'm glad you woke up," he whispers.

"What's wrong," she says.

"I don't know how to ask you."

"Go ahead."

"I want you to stay here in the city with me. I know it's crazy but I need help and you seem a kindred spirit and—"

She puts a finger to his lips.

"I'll stay," she says.

"You will."

"I'll help you," she says.

She puts her head on his chest and he is still thirsty when he finally falls back asleep. When he awakes the room is bright and Evey has dumped their bags out and he rolls over but Rebecca is gone.

♤

There are now less than twenty dollars in his wallet. Evey is banging together a toy car and a remote and now she is crying, hungry. He did not sleep well. But what did he expect. Rebecca was a stranger. Still, how much easier it could have been.

He digs through their belongings and finds a jar of green beans and she eats a few but then she'll eat no more. Perhaps it's all over.

She giggles as he changes her and he wonders if she's laughed at him before. He can't remember. He should know these things but for the stress of his existence.

He opens the blinds onto a highway. Billboards. Trucks. A swooping pigeon. He picks her up taking her away from the slobbered remote that she cries as he carries her to the bathroom. Her cries grow louder. He gives her lotion and shampoo bottles to play with but she will not stop crying. He puts down the toilet seat to do what he must and, "Please stop," he says but she will not and for the first time in how long he thinks she needs a mother. A thing known but now acutely felt. He's not sure how much longer he can go on like this, but he forces the thoughts out, the pity. To her cries he plans his next steps and she is still crying as the bathroom steams with his open-curtained shower and she is still crying as he bathes and changes her and she is crying what sounds like mama.

♠

Her face is red and she is huffing the remnants of her cries as they enter the lobby. The cushions of a small couch sag like a bowl. He rings the bell on the counter and waits and gives Evelyne a business card to teeth on.

An Indian woman with dark circles round her eyes emerges.

"Yes," she says, unsmiling.

"Room three cee," he says. "My wife and I would like to stay another three days."

"Let me check."

He has only seen two other guests. A suited man and his garish guest.

She looks at an old computer. "Smoking or none."

"No," he says, "I want to extend our stay in the room we already got." He hopes Rebecca has not checked them out.

"Which room."

"Three cee," he repeats.

She types on her computer.

"Yes," she says, "that is possible. Until when

will you be staying."

"What day is it today."

"Tuesday.

"Friday then," he says.

The keyboard clacks.

"Do you have a room key?" she asks.

"Yes," he says.

"What credit card?" she asks.

"Same one you have on file."

"One moment." She disappears down a hall. His heart pounds and when he looks down at Evey she is sucking on a pen. Her face is smeared with ink.

He is wiping her with his spit when the woman returns.

"Rebecca Alderman," she says, pushing a paper along the counter. "Sign here."

He looks at the woman. Then he signs the paper and slides it back.

"Checkout is eleven," she says.

"I know," he says.

♤

They are back in their room and he is sitting on the closed toilet debating. Evey squats on the floor pretending to read her favorite book. "Uh oh," she says. "Uh oh," she repeats. He has padded the rim of the bathtub with towels and any corners with blankets and he has closed the valve to the toilet and flushed it empty and secured it shut with duct-tape from his bag. The bathtub faucets are shut tight and he's removed all the soaps and shampoos and the hair dryer. On the floor beside her is a small bed he's formed from pillows and she has two sippy cups filled with water and there is an open container of sweet potato he's mashed for if there's one thing that horrifies him it's her choking. He has duct-taped the outlets and lubricated the doorknob with soap. Still, he'll block the door from outside.

He's clammy and his hands are shaking and his heart bangs and the mirror betrays his terror as he speaks what no parent ought.

She picks up her book and babbles and she is asking him to read.

He steps around her and double-checks the light switch though he's taped it on and he himself has trouble opening the door and she is watching as he closes it. He has not even finished his prayer when he hears her begin to cry. He feels like vomiting but he knows that if he doesn't leave now he'll not be able to do what he's reasoned he must. He thinks that if he were a better man he'd rather jail—but then he'd be leaving his daughter without a father. That man would be the coward. So he rationalizes as he pushes the chair against the bathroom door. He can hear her crying. Screaming: Papa. He stands there and then he grabs his bag and leaves.

His hand trembles. A Do Not Disturb sign sways. He can still hear her.

He enters again and paces furiously, grabbing his head and cursing and trying to hold back tears as he takes a sheet from the bed and stuffs it under the bathroom door. He takes the fitted sheet, lies this one near the room's door, and then leaves again. In the hallway he crouches and with a finger hooks the sheet and pads the door's gap while still trying to keep the sheet from sight. He listens. Her cries are muted.

He knocks on the door to the adjacent room. No one answers. But though she's inaudible, he still hears her as he trots down the hall and into the stairwell and down the stairs. His heart booming as he races across the lobby, pushing out the front door into a crisp air, cars horning and someone yelling but a babe's cries loud in his ears.

♤

"Stop," I said. "I don't want to know." I began to reach for my recorder but he placed his hand atop mine. It was the first time we'd touched. His hand was cold, hard, calloused.

He glowered.

"My life's been nothing but misery these past few months," I said, "and this ..."

He pulled the recorder away and he stood beside me. Tall, intimidating. "Who do you think you are."

I looked at him.

He finished his beer. "You'll listen so long as it does not offend your private sensibilities. But the moment it does you say, No more. Is that what you said to your friend. What was his name." He grimaced. "What kind of writer are you. You'll listen so long as it pleases but really you just sit there judging. Thinking that because you know the actions you know the man. But a man is more than the sum of his actions. A man can sleep and be the epitome of evil and a man can kill and be a saint. That's right. There will come a day when I stand before the law but only He can judge rightly for only He knows our private battles. The lunacy, the banging in our skulls.

"We can say I too have suffered and so I judge rightly, but then why does one man submit to the knife while another perseveres. Why is that. A man is born with his fortitude or without and he batters the doors of his ability and stretches his mettle only because he is so constructed. Grace is given, and the man who judges another for his lack blames the weaker for his constitution." He paused. "But just as the accused cannot be guilty for what was ordained, neither can the accuser be guilty for each of us is so constituted."

We looked at one another. He slapped the bar.

"You judge me as one gripped by infamy."

"Yes," I said, surprising myself, "because I could never do it. How could you—"

"You haven't been listening!" he shouted. "I'm telling you that given the day and the hour and all the moments previous you'd've even wiped your brow as I did for I chose the best given the permutations of my existence."

I shook my head. "No," I said. "No—"

"No!" he shouted. "You think that being in my shoes you'd've maintained the you called I, but facing the same repercussions—jail—you'd've turned the I of me. Easy to say you'd've done right, but faced with a cell's desiccation, what then." He glared at me. "If you could return a baby to its mother but the price tag was thirty years of your life would you do it." He looked at me.

Eventually, "No," I said.

"And if it were twenty?"

"No."

"Ten."

I shrugged.

"One."

I nodded.

"That's right. It depends. And so faced with the slow leakage of your life into prison's hellhole, you might turn your back. We are all of us calculating."

I stared at him. In truth, I wanted to know how his story ended. And though I was unsure of the nature of the man or the crime, I did not want him to leave. Whether there was any goodness within him I did not know.

He stood there, agitated. I had to use the bathroom but I did not move, fearful of breaking the spell holding him there. His face was red and I looked at his tattooed arm. Music played.

His eyes widened as though he'd just remembered something. Then he sat down and massaged his forehead and cleared his throat and spit into a napkin.

♤

Trucks rumble and horns bellow. Swallows twitter in violent chase but he swears he can hear her. His baby. His stomach hurts. Something is lodged within. He stands there. His whole body is beginning to tremor.

He runs back into the hotel and up the stairs and his hand shakes loose on the bones as he opens his door. Real cries displace those imaginary and he pushes aside the chair and carefully opens the bathroom door. She is curled on the floor crying so hard she cannot suck her thumb. He lifts and cradles her. An entanglement of moods and thoughts, mother, daughter, but those he cannot entertain for they will defeat him.

"I'm sorry," he whispers. "We'll find another way."

♤

He knows he does not have much time. He carries his bags and though Evelyne can waddle he carries her too.

He wanders Brooklyn's streets. Sun a spotlight: an old buttondown and jeans and he does not know who will hire him. Evey clings like a koala.

His boots clop down a street of abandoned stores. Sweatered men play dominos on a corner and they watch him and speak in Spanish and laugh. He has returned to this city to be close to Sarah. He passes For Hire signs and studies his reflection in a restaurant's dirty window: poorly dressed and unshaven and he envisions a grim future. Past his reflection a waiter emerges from the kitchen with a tray of food and his stomach grumbles. He checks his wallet and counts five dollars.

He looks up the street and recognizes a man approaching, a high school peer. He wants to laugh. A deus ex machina. He'll get a place to sleep and a babysitter and then he'll find low-pay work until he buys a new name. He'll learn a trade and stop living this hand-to-mouth existence that with each tragedy returns him to nothing. He'll teach Evey everything he knows and more he does not. He is shaking. Yet in quick succession comes the realization that the gears of communication will spin—his family, Sarah. He enters the tiny restaurant and heads to the black-shirted waiter pouring a cup of coffee.

"Can I use your bathroom."

The waiter nods to the back.

♤

No money, no food or plan. Evey is speaking to him in her strange tongue, holding his hand as she plods along the sidewalk. She wants him to let go so he does and she runs a few steps and falls and cries. He picks her up until she wants to walk again and then they replay the episode.

He finds a small park and he watches her play in the grass. Her mother is only miles away and he could end this now. He could take the subway and drop Evelyne with Sarah's neighbor and, leaving a note, disappear: I return your daughter on the condition that you never come find me. I love you both.

But he thinks that the State would still hunt him and he'd be on the run, only this time, alone. His stomach hurts. Evey plucks grass and sorts it and though it's the first time he's seen her do this he cannot enjoy it. He wants her to grow, to return his conversation. He tries to pick her up but she resists so he pulls her pink hat from his bag and straps it to her head and though the day is crisp he hopes her skin not already burned.

Later, they walk toward what seems their only option, their shadows in long exaggeration. He moves slowly and he pauses before an ice cream parlor and cannot remember the last time he splurged. He holds Evey in the crook of his arm.

"You want ice cream," he says.

Perhaps it's the first time she's heard the words.

He pushes open the door. A bell tingles above them.

"Hello," says a girl smiling from behind a counter.

He browses the flavors.

"What can I get you," says the girl.

"Vanilla cone," he says. "Two scoops."

He bounces Evey as they wait. More patrons enter.

"She's beautiful," says the girl, extending the cone.

He takes it and she punches buttons on the register.

"That'll be three fifty five," she says, straightening her visor.

He is about to give Evey a lick when he hands the cone back. Evey's face scrunches. People have lined up behind them.

"Can you hold this."

The girl takes it. Ice cream begins to dribble down her knuckles.

Balancing Evey and his bags, Savage takes out his wallet. He pays and takes the cone and she offers him his change but his hands are full and the ice cream is melting.

"That's for you," he says and turns to go. A boy opens the door for them.

"Thank you," he says.

He stands outside feeling like he's squandered a vast fortune. He is about to show Evey how to lick the ice cream when he realizes his mistake and heads back in. The bell dinging and ice cream melting until line receded he's back at the counter.

"You mind throwing some sprinkles on there."

The girl smiles. "Of course," she says. Evey watches greedily as the cone tilts.

"Shit," says the girl.

With bare hands she grabs the dropped scoops and he watches her throw them into the garbage. She prepares another.

"Here you are," she says.

Outside, Savage puts the ice cream to Evey's tongue and her mouth puckers from the cold. For a few minutes the two of them are happy.

♤

Time is a millstone. They've walked a half hour when finally they return to a place they passed earlier. He thought he would come up with something better but he has not.

It is early afternoon. A rusted sign above the door reads New Hope and the door is jammed but he pulls it open and a dark foyer gives onto a flight of stairs. He climbs.

A desk is labeled Intake but no one sits there. The walls are painted green and a hall drones its fluorescence and he comes to a small office in which a large woman sits. Puff-eyed and toad-mouthed. She spins her chair as though to face a window but there is only a wall. With a start she turns back.

"What're you doing here," she says. "We don't open until five."

"I'm sorry ma'am. The door was open."

"Jee-zus," she says, "someone must've broken the lock again." She sighs and tents her fingers. "Well?"

"I was always taught to pick myself up by my

own bootstraps."

"Young man," she says, "we don't open until five."

"Yes ma'am," he says and is heading down the hall when a shout comes.

He returns.

"Is that a baby?"

He looks at Evey. "She's almost two."

"Jee-zus," says the woman. She shakes her head.

She has him take a seat. The room contains little but a computer, filing cabinets, files. On her paper-strewn desk is a picture of two children and a plaque: God give me strength.

"Fill this out," she says and hands him a clipboard. He is taking it when he smells Evey. He's not sure he has more diapers.

"Where's the mother?" asks the woman, booting up her computer.

"Dead," he says.

She puts on glasses.

"I'm sorry to hear that," she says.

He nods and places Evey on the ground and hands her a small truck from his bag and she sits on the floor playing incalculable games while he fills in false information. Eventually he returns the clipboard.

She looks at the top paper. "Where did you live?" She places her glasses on her head.

"It burned down," he says.

"Where," she says.

"North Carolina," he says. "It's all gone, ma'am."

She looks at the paper and then she looks at Evey.

"Why're you here then?"

"I told you ma'am. It all burned down and me and my daughter—"

"No," she interrupts, putting the clipboard on her desk. "Why are you in New York?"

He speaks what he'd earlier rehearsed: "My mother used to lived here. But someone answered her door and said she'd gone. I asked where to and she said dead."

She studies him. Her golden placard reads Meredith Primrose.

"I asked her how come I'd not heard of the funeral." His eyes begin to well not from the death imagined but from his predicament. "She said because there'd been none to attend. The State had buried her and there was not even a headstone to visit because they buried her in a mass grave. I'd not spoken to my mother in five years."

She stares at him unmoved, a job in which trauma and evil are daily served.

She puts her glasses back on. "I'll need IDs for the both of you."

"Hers is gone," he says.

She looks to him. "You'll need something."

"It all burned," he says.

"A birth certificate. Something."

"Ok," he says. "I'll find something."

She enters information into her computer. "You'll be taken to another home on Thursday. They're better equipped there." Her glasses reflect her monitor. "A family shelter in Harlem."

"Harlem," he says.

"Yes."

"I was hoping to stay in Brooklyn, ma'am."

"It'll only be temporary until they can set you up in an apartment."

"An apartment."

"Yes," she says.

♠

The room in Brooklyn has a bed, a particle board desk, and a window onto the street below: cars and people and a leaking fire hydrant. He has towels and sheets and they have found his daughter a crib. But he cannot stay. He looks out the window. Evey tugs on his shirt.

"Uppa," she says.

He lifts her and kisses her forehead and they both look out together. Her breath steams the glass and he draws on it with his finger and she mimics him. They will go to the shelter in Harlem and he'll get a job and then he'll find them a room himself. Every ounce of charity he's accepted he's paid for in pride. Small price but he has little else. Dinner is brought to them.

♠

"What," said Savage, turning to me.

"Nothing," I said, though I was thinking about Alfred, old memories: Watching his wallet fall upwards from the top of an amusement park's loopty-loop. Trying to hang glide on a windless afternoon. The first time we kissed. The first time we made love. Savage stood to go.

"Where are you going?" I asked.

He shook his head and put money on the counter. "I've always been a good judge of character. And when I saw you I thought here is my vessel. Jesus." He fixed his belt and shook his head again. "You ever keep a secret."

I nodded.

"A real secret. And I mean keeping it even from her to whom omission is a lie."

I thought of Alfred.

"Of course you haven't." He watched the bartender take the money. "So you don't know what it is to keep one for twenty years. For a whole lifespan."

"Wait," I said, but the door opened and shut.

It was nearing evening and a writer's given such a story once in a lifetime. I rushed outside.

Cars raced a yellow light and a mother yelled at her child and a man sold balloons but I did not see Savage. If I lost him it would be forever, yet I was looking past a shouting drunk man when I spotted him, melancholy and tired.

I wanted to run but I'd drank too much.

He was ruminating. His head hanging and his hands fisted. I wanted to observe him but had the feeling that too much time gone, the loose bond between us would be reft. He would see me as a stranger. The sun glimmered fecund reflections in parked cars as I hurried to him.

He looked at me through the fugue of his thoughts.

"Savage," I said.

He nodded but kept on and I followed him and then he stopped and turned to look at me. Dark brown eyes, penetrating. He looked up the road and then down at his cowboy boots.

♧

In Harlem, they've given him a small room—
daycare and diapers and sheets and towels. By
small miracle the police have not yet come. He
has a nightmare: A snake wiggles from his ear. It
slithers round his neck and into his other ear and
chews on its own tail.

He has little time. Days, he thinks. He leaves
early and says goodbye to Evey at the small local
daycare and she has accustomed to his absence
and to strangers and this worries him.

Little is open. A diner and a few cafes and
bakeries.

"Perdown," he says, entering a deli.
"Trabajo."

A man fries eggs on a grill. He shakes his
head.

One place to the next. "Trabajo." Passing
Help Wanted signs to play his best odds with
those who look foreign, who might be illegally
working themselves. Sometimes they ask:
"Tienes identificación?" but he shakes his head
no. If he knew more Spanish he'd tell them he'd

work for nothing.

If he finds work and an apartment then he can go find Sarah, maybe even one day, after the pangs of retribution have subsided, let her see Evey. But it's strange that he's thinking on this when he sees her. A black dress and sneakers and hair straightened. Digging through her purse. He turns a corner and with his hands pocketed and shoulders hunched he quickens his pace. His heart is pummeling and the morning's cold and he can see his breath as he turns down an avenue and up another street and down more streets until seeing a dark-skinned man working a pick axe at the sidewalk he stops and says, "Mexicano."

The man sweats hunched over his work. A large scar runs down his arm.

"No," he says, "Dominicano."

Savage nods. "Trabajo," he says.

With drake eyes the man studies him and then he calls out for his jefe. Another man exits from the brownstone behind them, a plank ramp bonging beneath cement-dusted boots. The first man straightens himself and the two speak in a quick and undifferentiated Spanish.

The boss, his short curly hair glimmering from sweat, looks at Savage. "Seex doe-lars," he says.

"An hour."

"Jes," says the man.

Savage nods. He has worked for less.

"Jou have ID?"

Savage looks at the man.

"No," he says, "But I ... bueno trabajo."

The two men talk again and one tells a joke and they laugh. Savage is looking down the road for Sarah when the boss, taking a handkerchief from his pocket and dabbing his cheeks, addresses him again.

"Ok," he says. "My fren fine you ID."

Savage nods and then he looks up at the glassless windows of the house. He looks back down. "My daughter too. I need ID for my daughter."

The two men look at him.

Savage thinks. "Hija," he says. "ID for my hija."

The foreman puts the handkerchief back in his pocket.

"Ees no problem," he says.

THE FATTER

♠

They could come for him any moment. At the
shelter he is under a false name linked to at least
one crime. And what else had Vincent Laguria
already done. He cannot know.

Savage works at the bottom of construction's
pyramid. Replaceable labor, filling a
wheelbarrow with gutted wooden floor. Perhaps
they're already coming for him. He stacks the
planks and tries to heft the barrow but has to
take out weight and still too heavy he takes out
more. He thinks on Tom Herald, his new guise.
Alive or dead. Real or fake. He rolls the barrow
from the dusty diningroom into the hallway and
he puts it down and pulls off his facemask. His
thoughts are heavy.

♤

They do not come. He is told that the job will last a month and that if he works hard they'll take him on the next one. He tells the foreman he has to leave early to pick up his daughter from daycare and the foreman consents, tells him not to worry.

"Een thees ceety," he says, "there ees always work." The foreman wipes his forehead with the back of an arm, green with tattoo.

Savage is spent, but every afternoon he returns to find Evey waiting is a blessing. Each hug, smile, giggle, and diaper changed. And still they do not come. His muscles cramp and he cannot sleep for the fear—the badges and warrants—but after days, exhaustion accumulates, and he sleeps like a stone. Strange dreams. Mornings he'd rather not face.

♤

It is a cold Sunday. They are sawing by hand when Savage approaches the Dominican man. His name is Yared and he smokes a cigarette in the construction-zone livingroom. A radio plays. They are both covered in sawdust.

"Yared," says Savage. "Pregunta."

"Dígame, Tom." Smoke branches from his teeth.

"I need a room. Cuarto."

"Por cuanto tiempo."

Savage shrugs. "Three months."

Yared smiles. "No problem." He opens his hand, counts fingers. "Four cientos," he says. "One monf."

Savage nods. A sparrow lands and chirps on the window sill.

"My daughter," says Savage, "she will stay with me."

"Qué?"

"My daughter." He tries to remember. "Hija," he says.

Yared shakes his head. "No," he says, "solo

tú."

Savage nods. "My hija."

Yared pulls on his cigarette.

"I pay," says Savage, rubbing his fingers together.

Yared looks at him and then he flicks the butt of his cigarette at the sparrow.

"Quinientos," he says.

"Six," asks Savage.

Yared looks at him. Blows a cloud of smoke. "Jes," he says. "Six."

♤

They are ten living in the apartment and his room is shared, dark, humming by an old air conditioner. Three beds and a small foam pad. One bed is Yared's and is split with a cabbie who works nights. Savage and his daughter move in silence.

The apartment has a livingroom, a television, a kitchenette, and a bathroom. Mostly it's empty for everyone works. Men and women the lubricant of our society. The shift laborers. There's a little girl who lives with her parents and uncle in another room and the two girls become friends, the girl and his daughter: Magnificent Harold. So her social security card says now.

He doesn't know what's become of them, Magnificent and Thomas Harold. Whether they're dead or their identities were stolen or sold or whether they ever existed at all. He'd prefer ignorance and sometimes at night he prays they not be real. But eventually he stops for there is nothing to which we cannot accustom. He calls his daughter Maggie.

♤

He gets a day off every two weeks and on this day he feels no guilt at leaving Maggie at daycare and it is drizzling and warm as he walks across town. From inside a cafe he watches commuters. Sips coffee. Later, he steps in puddles and the rain dampens his baseball cap. A shaved head, tanned skin, blue contacts, a beard. Has tried to change what little he can. Eventually he arrives.

He enters a diner. A long counter and a few booths and an ill-tempered waiter. He sits and orders food and when the table by the window opens up he gets up and takes it. He doffs his hat and looks out—the building's entrance, her window. He leafs a book but he does not read. He needs the bathroom but he just crosses his legs and dabs at the crumbs of his sandwich.

More weeks to repeat the same, days of leisure coming and going like fractals. He sits turning a page and he's taking a bite of a tuna melt when there's movement in his periphery. A feeling he remembers:

They lie in bed, a guillotine of sun crossing

the room. He lotions her belly.

"Marry me."

She stares up at their leak-stained ceiling.

"No."

"Please, for me, for my family."

"Never," she says, kissing him. "Not by shotgun or pistol."

"Please."

"No," she says angrily.

Now, he looks out the window and she is ascending the stairs. Jeans and t-shirt and her hair in a wrap and he wonders if she still lives there or if she only goes to check the mail, the answering machine. He wonders what she does for work. She is searching her bag. Maybe she is summoning her will. The weight of a lost child like a yoke.

♤

Maggie is in a yellow raincoat and hat and she is talking about her fifth birthday. Her skin has gilded and her hair had grown feral until a horrified beautician had shown him to braid it. Rain hammers their umbrella. Bulked, an arm tattooed black, earrings, bleached hair, a nose ring, he holds her hand as she stomps puddles and blabbers about all the things a big girl can do. Shop and cook and drive. To see his patience is to know love.

They wait at a corner for the light. Rain pipples. She looks up with eyes the color of tea. "I can go to school by myself when I'm five. Right, daddy?"

"No," he says. "Not till you're ten."

She takes her hand from his and begins to count, uncurling little fingers.

"But that's a long time!" she yells.

He nods. "Yes it is, baby."

She extends her hand to him and he takes it and when they cross the street she is talking about what she can do when she is ten—go to school alone and marry.

By the time they've arrived it's stopped raining. The air's steamy. A long puddle slicks the playground and reflects the columned building before them. Children and parents slosh through.

"It's my school!" she shouts and starts running up the stairs.

"Hold on," he calls and closes his umbrella and takes her hand and they enter together.

A long fluorescent hallway through which his umbrella taps. At a table he shows a woman the paper he'd been mailed. She takes it. He watches. Worries that they've been waiting, this counterfeit.

"Ms. Lefferts," she reads. "Room one sixteen. End of the hall make a right."

"Thank you, ma'am," he says and they head on, Maggie towing him to her classroom.

♤

The diner, the coffee, the sandwich, sitting by the window. It's cold. A paper turkey sits on the table. Would that Sarah knew. What rage would be borne on him.

He is eating and reading when just past the fogged window she appears. Her hair wild in the wind. Her hand cups round a flame. Her eyebrows. The arc of her nose. A cigarette's ember and a feather of smoke. She flicks a burning match.

He claws his book and does not move and a fly lands on his plate as she exhales smoke. He wonders how long she's been smoking and then he wants her to see him. To end this. Perhaps that's why he's come.

"Can I get you anything else?" A waiter stands beside him. "Sir?"

The waiter clears his throat.

Finally: "Go away," says Savage, speaking to the window.

The diner door opens but he watches her. Watches and remembers. A great divide within himself.

♤

He feels as though he has never made a decision.
As though he watches a great play. Not a
commentary on life but life itself.

The bar had loudened and Savage's story was competing with others. Conversations I'd rather not have heard but could not help for their shouting. The bartender welcomed regulars, some of who sat and listened and left, but I looked at Savage. Drowned out by the less important.

THE FATHER

♤

Months and years and he sits in an auditorium's last row. He was late out of work and therefore late to bring her here but in truth he is nervous. He feels he's living on borrowed time.

He sits in darkness watching the stage. Faces half-shadowed by amateur lighting. Feet unlit that the children seem an apparition. Maggie raises her clarinet and Savage tears for the beauty of it. Junkyard horns would have pleased him.

At home, by dim lamp, they eat Chinese takeout. A room that is kitchen and livingroom and diningroom all. In an aquarium, a small turtle tumbles over a plastic log.

Savage is basking in pride when Maggie asks: "Why don't I have a mother?"

He swallows.

She slurps up a noodle. A finger glints the nickel ring she begged him to buy.

"I loved your mother," he says.

"I know." She chews as though on a thought

and then sips her soda. "But maybe you can love someone else. Maybe mama would want that."

He puts down his chopsticks. A picture of them hangs on the wall.

"Maybe," he says.

"Maybe what."

"Maybe it's not her consent that bothers me."

"I want you to be happy." She begins to clear the table. This tiny adult. "I see you sometimes, Papa." She stacks plates and is about to take his when he stops her.

"And how do I look," he says.

She takes food cartons to the counter.

He turns: "Tell me," he says.

She tosses garbage.

"I never kept anything from my father," he says.

She takes ice cream from the freezer and serves two bowls and places one before him. "You seem lonely," she says.

♤

Katia is tall, Ukrainian, a secretary, and much of what he's told her is a lie. Yet such has been his survival. No guilt for his breath, thirst, hunger. Only one farce that pains him and for that he pays his penance. In his private conversations with God he begs for mercy.

They met at a bar. She stepped on his foot and that night, lying naked on her floor, he told her his false history. The next time he saw her he did not remember what he'd said.

Six months pass and they climb the stairs to his apartment. Katia carrying a foiled tray of *plov*, his keys jangling to unlock the door but it opening first. Maggie standing there in a dress.

They sit at the table. The pale, brunette Ukrainian and the tattooed man and the brown child eating beneath an eighth-grade poster about cells. Katia teaches them Russian: plate and bread and spoon and love.

"So," says Katia, wiping her mouth, "what do you want to be when you grow up?"

Maggie smiles. "A historian."

Savage puts down his fork. He's heard this before.

"We don't have any pictures of my mother. Right, Papa?"

He places his elbows on the table and clasps his hands.

Maggie turns to Katia. "They all burned when the house caught fire."

Here is why he's never brought a woman home.

"I want to preserve things and tell their stories."

Katia smiles. "Have you looked on the internet?"

"For what?" asks Maggie.

"A picture."

Savage stands and clears the table. The others balance their glasses and silverware atop their plates, carrying their loads to the sink where Savage begins to wash.

"We looked. Right, Papa?"

He scrubs the plates too hard.

"Yes," he says.

"Oh but there must be something." Katia opens a cupboard. "In the local newspaper maybe or how do you say, a obituary—"

Savage bangs a plate onto the dish rack. A glass shatters and the three stand there, the faucet running and the cupboards open and Maggie holding the fridge door.

♤

He remembers something else. Fishing on a charter boat with Maggie. The sea choppy.

A fish radar blips and her pole bends and looking at the radar Maggie pulls Savage in close and whispers: "Papa, we're cheating."

He helps her pull in another shimmering sea bass and the boat's captain tears the hook from its mouth and heaves the fish into the large cooler so crammed it won't shut. The fish gapes for water, suffocating. Maggie stares wide-eyed.

"Papa," she says, "he's screaming."

The stout captain asks her to sit on the cooler to keep it closed and her face pales. Beneath her, entombed fish bat their tails as she sits there weeping.

The boat shuttles them back to the harbor, waves whacking its bow, spraying. Savage holds his daughter's hand as she sits atop the large cooler.

"It's ok," he says.

"They're dying," she says. The sun glittering her tears and prisming the vast water. "Papa, I don't want to go fishing again." The cooler thumps beneath her.

"Ok," he says.

"And I don't want to eat them."

"Ok."

She squeezes his hand. "No animals, Papa. None."

He nods. Seagulls circle above them. How he loves her.

THE FATHER

♤

A curious family. Savage and Katia and the precocious daughter. Katia comes over often and the two, Katia and Maggie, go for manicures. An eleven-year-old with French tips. Concessions made for what Savage deems happiness. Rhythms, boundaries, Katia moves in. She brings what she owns and tosses what's his. A couch in which he cannot get comfortable. The trappings of domesticity. He begins to forget. Easy omens.

♤

He sat there contemplating to the bar's music, its darts, and shouting. His beer was almost empty and I was about to speak when, "We didn't last," he said. "I was too happy." He rubbed his temples.

"I don't want you to take this the wrong way," I said.

Another beer arrived and he took a sip.

"But for all this talk of an extraordinary life, yours was normal."

He chuckled. "That is the irony," he said. "That my circumstance forced me to be mediocre. Working like a dog just for sustenance. I welcomed security." He shook his head. "I became complacent under Katia's watch. But I did not trust happiness."

He drank.

"I'll tell you a story," he said. "One day, watching Katia and Maggie play Scrabble on the livingroom floor, something began to grow inside me. I sat on the couch with a book but I was watching them. Play hard, crush me, Katia was saying and I was sitting there brimming with something I soon realized love. Now I don't know if I'm a sentimental man because I've yet to meet a man who is not, but it was roiling and boiling bursting within me. The love." He smacked his lips. "So powerful and encompassing I felt at its mercy and it felt like grace. That despite the suffering I'd caused, I'd not slipped from God's hand. A love so overpowering I began to weep. Listening to Katia's groans at another of Maggie's triple-word plays and feeling a renewed surge, I thought I would break. That I'd drop to my knees for He had visited upon me, a lowly sinner whose greatness had been measured only in pain. I was ready to repent—exploding with love, so feeling every hair on my body, every nerve and pore, that I was ready to confess everything—that her mother lived nearby and that her name was not Maggie and that I'd kidnapped her." He smiled. "The two of them looked up and Maggie said, Papa are you ok, and I said, Yes, baby, daddy's fine, but I have something to say—and I was opening my mouth about to unveil the heinous infrastructure of her upbringing when a bird smacked into the window." He clapped his hands. "Maggie ran over and looked out and said, It's dead, Papa. The bird is dead." He gave a strange smile. "A sparrow flung from the pinky nail of God."

♠

The diner's staff smile and call him by assumed name for they do no know what he's about. How many years it has been. Ten? Watching Sarah this whole time, he thinks recently her belly has been growing.

He blows on his coffee. Could she still think him returning? He takes a book from his coat. She's not wrong, he thinks. I've stayed close.

He reads and then his head angles and he watches. Those days when he spies her, he's jolted back to that moment when he'd packed a bag and left. Thinking he was deciding then, doing, but no longer. He feels himself a spectator, audience to his own life.

Outside the sky is gray and pedestrians pass hunched, breathing into collars, rubbing their arms. A tree's gone to orange and it loses leaves with a gust of wind. Savage burns his tongue.

"Damnit," he blurts, putting the mug down, coffee sloshing.

He is sopping it up with a napkin when a bell rings behind him and it strikes him how little he thinks about her. How at night, no longer tormented, he falls into sleep's grave like a dead man. Nor does he think of her on awaking. A phantom evoked only by circumstantial amalgamation—perfume, a lilt, an intonation—she has haunted him little of late.

He is signaling but the waiter passes him and heads to the entrance.

"Just one," says the voice behind him.

He takes a sharp breath. He covers his face with his hand.

The waiter and patron brush past him. That inimitable scent. He swallows.

She says Thank you and he can just make out the figure at the diner's end, easing herself into a booth. She is pregnant.

His hands are sweaty and he is feverish and he worries that he is making himself conspicuous. He berates himself for not having seen her. She looks at a menu.

His head is shaved and work has added heft to his frame and he has grown his beard and he wears long sleeves. He hides the name tattooed on his finger. He must look different, but what guise is there for the man within? Idiosyncrasies of the spirit are a thumbprint. She will see him.

"Your food'll be out shortly," says the waiter.

Savage nods.

Now he can see her ordering. He cowers into his book, turns a page with trembling hands. His senses are sharpened: the smell of french fries and hamburgers, the cash register's dings. Yet if he's so attuned then why doesn't he notice the meal placed before him and the waiter asking if there'll be anything else.

"No," says Savage, a part of him already knowing.

She has stopped moving. She has spotted him.

He turns to face her and their eyes span a decade and in recognition everything is present, departure and return are joined. Yet the ego quickly reconstructs, turns memory to brick, and across the restaurant's tables, her gazed is constructed by horror and by rage.

She screams but he runs like a man on fire.

III

♤

His chest is heaving and he moves tautly in his curtain-drawn room. Sweat dampens his shirt and trickles into his eyes. I have done this before, he tells himself. A snared fox chewing off its foot.

He packs little. A sweater and a book and all the underwear and socks he can cram. He chides himself for not having this bag ready. He got comfortable, careless. He packs toiletries and t-shirts and an electric razor and his knife and from a drawer he takes banded wads of money. He thought he'd had more.

It will look like a man who's left in a rush but that does not matter now. He wishes he had a gun but for what. Still, he wishes it.

The drawer is angled open as he carries an empty suitcase and his duffel into his daughter's room. He looks around and this is what he's been dreading. He should have done this first. He shuts the blinds and turns back round. Posters and books and stuffed animals and a radio. Everything meticulous. This is her home. He carefully places the suitcase on her bed and opens it and in its mesh pocket is the missing money. He shoves one band into a pocket, another into his boot, another into his coat. He weighs the last one and then he puts it back in his daughter's suitcase. He stands there for a moment, this strange cowboy, and then he takes another wad from his bag and puts it in her suitcase too.

An old calculus runs through his mind. How long does he have. Sarah, the police, the FBI. He heads to his daughter's mirror. He is a stranger unto himself, but Sarah has seen him.

With the suitcase still open and the razor's cord dragging, he returns to his room to dig through his closet. From its bottom he pulls out a large plastic bag unopened in years. Artifacts from old times. He wishes he'd not lost so much of it, the fear.

He takes the plastic bag into the bathroom and pulls the light's chain and closes the door. He places the bag into the sink and opens it. Wigs and contacts and shaving cream and razors and costume mustaches and clip-on earrings and skin tanner and hats and glasses. He puts the bag on the floor and takes off his shirt and muscles glistening he plugs in the razor. It rattles as he shaves his head bent over the sink. Maybe they'll set up check points. Maybe I'll be on the news. But they don't know my alias. I have some time.

He lathers his head with shaving cream. Uses a disposable blade. Beads of blood.

"I don't know what I'll tell her," he says aloud, rinsing the razor, tapping it.

He looks up. His head is stippled red and he

is mossed by his shorn hair. He showers and towels himself off and then he puts on a wig. He worries that the contacts are old but their sting soon subsides. "I have time," he says to himself.

He sifts the mustaches but then he looks in the mirror and remembers his beard and decides to shave himself clean. He rinses off again in the shower that the wire-framed glasses he chooses are fogged. He dresses and when he's done he looks at himself. Blonde and blue-eyed, younger, effeminate. Still, there is that we cannot hide.

He grabs the bag and the razor and now he moves with a rush he'd earlier restrained. Beasts of his nature. He stuffs her bag with things she'll later not want and forgets things she'll later need and when he's done the suitcase will not close. He removes things at random left crumpled on the floor and taking one last look around he grabs the stuffed dog Sarah'd given her, only remembrance, and shoves that in too. He speaks soliloquies to none but himself.

He puts on a coat and with his duffel bag shouldered and her suitcase under his other arm he hurries down the hall. The bathroom light is still on but it does not matter. He maneuvers down the stairwell, banging the walls with their luggage as he descends. In the dark vestibule he puts the suitcase down to unlock the door and he is opening it when suddenly he realizes what he is about and he is about to laugh and then he does. His plan is mad. He would have to show up to Maggie's school like this, with bags, in disguise. He shuts the door.

♤

A silent dinner. Maggie sits across from him eating undercooked pasta and burned sauce and staring at his bald head. She has seen her packed suitcase. He'd once told her of all their moves but she remembers none of them. Only the hazy memory of a bus ride. The radiator wheezes.

"Papa," she says, putting down her fork, "where are we going?"

"I don't know," he says.

She looks at her plate.

"I don't want to go."

"I know," he says, leaning on his elbows. "But we have to."

"Why." A tear plips into her bowl of food. "I'll miss my friends."

Above them a moth flaps in the light shade. The light flickers.

"You'll make new friends."

She shakes her head. "And what about school?" Her eyes rim with tears.

"Listen," he says, "I don't want to leave either, but daddy lost his job."

The light shade tinkles above. He looks up. The moth stills.

"You can't do this," she says. "You cant ... like I'm a ... a ...." She chokes on her words.

"Drink water, baby."

She does not.

The dead moth casts an arrowhead's shadow. Savage clears his throat.

"Listen," he says. "To hurt you is to hurt myself. Remember your fever last year. The hospital. The saline drip. Your fever so high you were crying mommy even though she's gone."

She shakes her head.

"Well I do. I do remember. You were tearing my heart out and I told God that if he had to take one of us that it be me because you're the reason I exist. You're why I'm here. We am one. Do you understand."

She does not respond.

"You're the greatness I'd always imagined for myself. And you are mad at me now and perhaps you should be—if there were another path I would take it—but this is what must be done. Your father lost his job, and he must find another."

She looks up. "But why can't we stay and find another job here?"

Every story he has concocted has failed the litmus test of his imagination.

"There are things your father has done which he cannot undo. They'll be looking for me."

She looks up. Inquisitor eyes. "Who."

"The police," he says.

"Did you do something bad?"

He does not answer, then, "Yes," he says.

"What did you do."

"A thing I cannot take back. It was done a long time ago."

"What did you do, Papa? Did you kill someone?"

Perhaps he should answer: Yes, I killed a mother, but, "No," he says, "no I did not."

"Is it bad, Papa? What you did?"

He looks at her. "Yes," he says, "it was bad."

She looks down at her plate as though studying. The moth casts her in shadow. Then she looks up and stands. She leaves the room and her door shuts and he is left alone with the radiator's tinny percussion. When she returns she is holding something. He blows his nose.

"What is it," he says.

She opens her hand. A ring glints, its tiny diamond biggened by the palm that holds it.

He looks at it. Then at her.

"I'm sorry," she says. Her eyes sparkle.

He nods and takes it and weighs it in his hand. So much smaller than he'd remembered.

She is crying.

He takes her in his arms and holds her.

"I stole too," he says. "Something very valuable."

"Can you give it back?"

"No," he says.

He holds her for some time and then she pushes away.

"I'll go with you, Papa," she says. "I just want to be with you."

He tells her he needs to go for a walk and she asks to accompany him but he says no. She pleads but he is insistent and he is trundling down the stairs when he yells up: "Don't turn the tv on."

Outside the night is cold and he walks with a hat and sweatshirt, bundled though adrenaline keeps him warm. If he knew of the dispatches, of his picture being televised on how many tens of thousands of screens, he would be more worried, but he does not know and does not bother imagining.

Pools of lamplight and the blue-glowing windows of those sitting to television and he feigns ignorance of his destination. But it is an old instinct on which he acts for this is his goodbye.

A police car passes but it speeds up and races through a red light. If he looked up he would notice the flyers.

He walks on for a half hour until he arrives. The diner glows by a neon sign and across the street is the apartment he has surveilled for years. In its dim window is a figure and he is looking up, begging forgiveness, when the figure begins to turn toward him. He quickens his step and is rounding a corner when he sees a paper taped to a lamp pole. No one watches so he tears it down and thrusts it into his pocket. He is blocks away when he unfolds it: His picture. His crime. Hurrying home, he sees many of them.

THE FATHER

♤

The moon hangs like a spider egg. A cold wind and they, father and daughter, hunker down the sidewalk. The daughter rolling her suitcase, her mother's ring sparkling on her thumb. The father wearing a blonde wig, hefting his duffel bag, and the two of them in single file, breaths contrailing behind them.

They arrive at the building close to eleven. They climb the stairs and Savage rings the bell but a strange man answers.

"Is Yared here," says Savage.

The man is dressed in a stained t-shirt and instead of answering he shuts the door. Under the stoop's orange light they wait and Savage is about to ring again when the door opens. Yared, the construction worker, stands with a beer in his hand.

"I need a favor," says Savage.

He sucks his teeth. "Jou can't to live here no more."

"It's not that." Savage leans in. "I need to borrow your car."

Yared tries to sip his beer but it's empty. He shakes his head. "No," he says and starts to close the door but Savage pushes it back.

"I just need your car." Savage points at an old car parked on the street. "I'll pay you."

Yared looks past Savage.

"Hola, hermosa."

"Hi, Yared," replies Maggie.

"Como ha crecido," he says.

"Please," says Savage.

Yared looks at him. "Lo ví en las noticias."

"What?"

"The news." Then, "Lo ví," he whispers.

Savage pales but he pretends not to understand.

"I'll pay you," he says. "Amigo. We're amigos. And I need your car and I'll pay you for it. Money. Deenayro."

Yared stands there looking at him. Maggie's in his shadow.

Savage takes out a wad from his coat. A thousand dollars though he would pay more for a car worth less. He extends it. Yared looks at it. Then suddenly Yared snatches it and closes the door.

Savage is standing there staring at a handprint begrimed in the door's paint when he starts to feel rage. A rage that would raze a building and end a life and he starts banging on the door, yelling, and he is scaring his daughter when the door opens again to Yared holding a key.

♤

He drives without map but simple destination:
south. Cones of light clocking their progress and
Maggie sleeping in the passenger seat beside
him. The car rattles and pushing fifty it shrieks
but she does not wake. Her head leans on the
door, her fist pressed to her chin, a tendril of
drool. She snores. He drives. The city's twinkling
skyline shrinks behind them and fiery towers of
industry give unto a forest zippered by highway.
The car's exhaust fans out.

He stops for gas and adds oil and cleans the
windshield and goes to pay and when he returns
she is still sleeping. Digging through his bag, he
drops money to the car's floor among the trash
littered there but he will get it later. For now he
covers his daughter in a sweatshirt and the
engine hammers and he drives on, their dim
headlights tweezing the night before them.

When the sun rises they are traveling through
fields furrowed and seeded and picketed with
signs: watermelon and tomato and corn and soy
and cotton. The sky above them is aflame.
Maggie yawns and looking out she asks where

they are.

"Virginia," he says.

"Where are we going?"

"North Carolina," he says. "To see my family."

She looks out at single-story homes. Then she looks at the ring she wears on her thumb.

"You lied to me," she says.

"Yes," he responds.

For a while they drive in silence, a neon dawn banding their backdrop. He sees her tapping at the door handle.

"Papa," she says, "you can't lie to me anymore."

He turns to look at her. He is on his third coffee.

"Ok," he says.

She puts her feet on her seat and hugs her legs.

"Papa, that means you have to tell me everything." She leans her head on her knees, turns to face him. "Not telling someone is the same as lying."

"Who told you that," he says.

"You did."

He turns back to the road. A car passes them. Another.

"Ok," he says, but he does not speak again for a long time. He debates. Across a vast plantation he sees the ocean. Billboards for cheap fireworks and cigarettes. Finally he speaks.

"There are some things I can't tell you yet." He reaches for his cold coffee and sips it and places it back in the rickety cup holder. "You must be patient. And I know what I ask of you—patience—is not easy, for you are a child and what I ask would tear a man apart. But you must know that I love you and everything I've done has been for you." He looks at her and then back at the road. "My sole purpose is you. You are my greatness."

He drives on and she says nothing for she knows that he will continue and he does.

"I have a family. A mother and a father and two sisters. And since I ran from them I've lived under the threat that one day a knock would come at our door and someone would take you from me. There is no chasm of time across which your past will not reach. But now we return because perhaps they will have forgiven me."

She watches the road ahead. "What did you do."

"I cannot tell you yet. But I will. When you are eighteen and old enough to decide if your father deserves incarceration pity or accolade. You can choose to leave me then."

"I won't leave you, daddy," she says.

"We will see," he responds.

They drive on and she is unzipping the backpack at her feet when she stops and looks up.

"Papa," she says.

"Yes, darling," he says.

"Is mama still alive?"

"No," he says.

♤

He has parked them in the driveway of an empty beach house and has told her he may have to change his name. If a cop approaches them he'll say he's waiting on a friend and if they ask for his ID he will give it and pray.

Through their open windows they can hear the ocean. Cool air. White dunes. Maggie asks if they can go to the beach, she is tired of sitting, but he says they must wait. He watches the house across the street.

"Papa. Papa."

The sun is much higher.

"Papa."

He jolts upward but it is not the police of his dream.

"Papa, look."

She points. Across the street a car has parked and a woman has exited and it is his eldest sister: Agnes.

♤

He looked at me with eyes gone dim as though a mind still peopled by the memory.

"I had to go back," he said.

The bar was so loud we leaned into one another like old companions though this man, Savage, knew nothing of me. He sat so close I could smell the sweetness of his breath.

"What else could I have done," he said. He shook his head. "Each man is given only so many repetitions. So many ice cream cones and skydives and chili peppers before the body or mind or life itself says no, enough." A woman crowded us trying to order a drink. I changed the tape and hoped my recorder was still working.

"I couldn't restart anymore," he said. "Not with Maggie. It'd been difficult to uproot a baby, yet it was only the essentials I'd had to consider. Diapers and formula and food, but I did not have to suffer another's anguish or trepidation or will. Hers had been primal needs—food, shelter, water—but they became higher wants—security and stability and friendship and love. And I couldn't do it again. I couldn't. So I returned to the cradle of my youth, to the very house in which I'd been born, sitting on the ocean's edge like a challenge to Mother Nature."

THE FATHER

♠

Maggie stands behind him as he knocks on the
door screen, baggage in hand. He hears the cry of
a seagull and then footsteps. A sky clear as
plastic. The ocean's slaps.

The door opens and Agnes stands there—
older, larger, a double chin.

"What're you thinking banging like that.
What do you want."

She does not recognize him. He takes off his
hat, his wig, his glasses, and her hand on the
door falls to her side.

She says his name. He pushes his daughter
forward.

"This is Maggie," he says.

She looks at the child and she does not stop
looking. Her eyes well and now she looks up at
Savage, gridded by the screen. "Daddy's dead,"
she says.

Inside: sun-faded paintings, cheap couches, a
glass table atop a ship's wheel. A muggy darkness
in which a fly buzzes.

"Give your aunt a hug," he says and Maggie does.

"Your father's old room is in the back," says Agnes.

Maggie tugs at Savage and he leans down and kisses her head. "Go on and play."

She heads off and this world to her is a mystery.

♠

They sit at the dining table drinking sweet tea.
Agnes tells him about the last months of their
father. Each detail a personal blow. She offers
him tissues and tells him of their mother's life
and hers and their sister's and the hole his
disappearance has left. He wonders why he's
come. Memories return and a fly lands on his
finger and he flicks it off. The room smells of
mothballs.

"I don't know if you should stay here," she
says.

On the table are porcelain shakers, cherubs.
He picks one up.

"You caused a lot of suffering."

He looks down at the mound of pepper he's
making with his fidgeting. "We ain't got no place
to go."

She rubs her glass and then she reaches
across the table to place her hand on his to stop
the shaking. "Maybe you can come stay with me
in Virginia. We have an extra room."

Their hands clasp.

"That is a great kindness you'd be doing me," he says.

She grips him harder. "You're my brother and I only got the one."

He tries to smile and then he lets go of her hand and shakes his head. "No," he says. "I can't put this on you." He brushes the pepper off the table. "I can't make you pay what you don't know the cost of."

Her head cocks.

"What," he says.

"Nothing," she says, but when he turns round, Maggie is peeking from the hallway.

♤

He holds a framed picture of his father holding up a large fish. Savage might have written him, called, anything.

He replaces the picture and sits back down at the diningroom table. His sister has taken Maggie out and he is listening to a clock. The sky is turning and a beer sits before him but he does not drink.

The door opens.

"Why're you sitting in the dark," says Agnes, holding groceries, flicking a switch.

"Papa!" shouts Maggie. "Look." She runs over and shows off her arms plastered in fake tattoos.

Agnes places the groceries on the counter and turns on the television. Savage stands to change the channel.

"But Papa you didn't see all of them." She tugs on him as he flips channels. "Papa, look."

"Put it back on the news," says Agnes, arranging food in the refrigerator. He leaves the tv on an old western.

She looks over the fridge's door. "I asked you

to put on the news."

"Watch it later," he says.

"Papa, look."

"Yes, baby." He kisses her head and leaves her standing there to go sit and take up his beer. It's gone warm.

"You didn't even look!" she shouts over gunshots, Indians.

"Can you at least turn that down?" calls Agnes.

"Maggie," he says, but she turns the volume up and storms down the hall.

Agnes unpacks.

"She was excited to see you," she says. "You should've paid her mind."

He drinks and stands and turns down the volume and then he heads down the hall. Old memories as he stands in the doorway to his room. Faux wooden paneling and posters and airplane models hanging by fishline. Maggie is crouched on the floor reading an old comic. She is beautiful. She turns a page and he thinks he should apologize and sit beside her but he does not. He keeps down the hall and unlocks a door onto the beach. Dusk and mist and a short wooden walk. He heads to its end and stands in a small gazebo. Pelicans, starlings, soon the crabs. Dark water glinting.

When he hears the door open he does not turn for he thinks it Maggie. He will tell her the names of things and if the two of them are still here in the morning he will take her fishing again, will make her. But the voice that comes is different.

"You came back."

He keeps looking out to the sea for despite how often he's planned this moment his father is dead. A family of five whittled to three and now him prodigal.

"Yes," he says.

She stands next to him. The cry of a seagull like something unsheathed.

He can smell her and he leans against the rail and she places her hand on his. Veiny, spotted, bony. He turns. Her cheeks have caved and her eyes are worn. Behind her, the window to his old bedroom silhouettes his daughter. Strands of his mother's white hair flutter in the wind.

She studies him and pulls up his sleeve and touches his dark tattoo. "I barely recognized you," she says, holding his wrist. "You missed your father's funeral."

She touches his hair and speaks in a voice almost forgotten. "He wouldn't stop asking about you. Every time the phone rang or somebody knocked."

He takes his hand from hers and zips his coat, stuffs his hands into his pockets. No way to bring back the man or the child lost.

"I had to be the one to always tell him. It's not your son. He lay on his deathbed and I had to tell him you'd never come. That you'd strayed from the path of God." She smiles softly. "He lay there and took my hand and we prayed for you. Your father was dying and he was praying for you. Bless his heart."

She looks at the ocean. A cupola of moon rising. The screen door opens again.

"Papa? Can I come out?"

His mothers leans in. "The last thing he said was that if you returned I should call the police. That your guilt is too much for any man and the law is not justice but it will do."

"So they haven't even called yet," asks Savage.

They can hear Maggie's footsteps crossing the wooden walkway.

His mother shakes her head. "I leave justice between you and God."

♤

It's decided they'll stay for a week while his sister
prepares her home and one late night Savage is
making a sandwich in the kitchen when his
mother enters dressed in a nightgown, looking
like she's not slept in days. She stands and stares
and then goes back to her room. The next day
she does not remember doing it.

He and Maggie only leave the house to go to
the beach. They spend much of their time in
silence. Day by day she reminds him more of her
mother.

The fall unfolds: cold sand, the ocean
reflecting the dawn. A cup of coffee steams in his
hand and the fishing pole his daughter holds
arches with the waves. She is not happy but at
least they kill nothing. She reels in and he
watches her struggle with a small spot fish,
screaming as she grabs it and it puffs and pricks
her. The spot flops on the sand and he tells her to
step on it to work out the hook. Her hair flares in
the breeze.

"You do it, Papa," she cries, but he will not.

Eventually she gets the fish off and she throws it into the water and they watch it dart into a wave. She wants to go back inside but he makes her stay longer. Cries as she does. And the sun casts shortening shadows until they head back in for grandmother's breakfast. Bacon and eggs and pancakes and it is more than they can eat.

He sits at the table cleaning his teeth with a toothpick and he watches them clear the table. A quiet and sturdy love growing. Maggie tells her grandmother about her old school and then she asks about her mother, if she knew her.

Her grandmother looks at Savage. "No," she says.

♤

They stay for a day more, two, for perhaps this .
visit will be their last. One afternoon his mother
arrives from shopping with Maggie, the two
laughing, happy, when Savage is standing there
with packed bags.

"We've been here too long. People'll ask
questions. Miracle they haven't come already."

"You don't have to leave yet," says his mother,
putting down the groceries.

"The phone kept ringing. We knew this would
come," he says.

Maggie holds back tears.

He puts down the bags and kneels and takes
her hands. "Baby, if you want to stay, it's ok. We
will always be partners you and me no matter the
distance. But they'll come for me here. And if
they do they will take me away."

But what child would leave the parent. And
what parent would present such a choice.

Her eyes start to glimmer and his heart will
break at what unknown futures she imagines.
Now she is shaking and now she is crying and

now she is holding him. "Why do you want to leave me, Papa? What did I do?" she screams. "Why do you want to leave me!" She is crying like nothing he's ever heard. Her throat going hoarse as he holds her.

♠

A bus crosses a long bridge over water tinfoiled by sun. It drives through fields and forest and, holding a stuffed dog, Maggie sleeps on his shoulder. He listens to the squeak of the bus' brakes and its shocks and to her breath.

Later, they take a taxi down a suburban street in Virginia and arrive at his sister's house, a bigger home than he'd imagined. Green shutters and a brick chimney. Tall trees leaning over a stone-tiled roof and his sister and her family standing on the porch.

Holding his daughter's hand, he shades his face and they head up the walkway.

♤

The bar was dark and I wondered how many hours we'd been there.

"Weren't you scared of being caught? Of the police finding you? Of your sister and her family telling the wrong—"

"Yes," he interrupted, "I lived in a constant fear. Till things settled down and I got a new name and job and we moved."

"What was your new name?"

"Christian Savage," he said.

I looked at him.

"And your daughter's?"

He stared at his empty glass.

"Small miracle," he said. "Same first name. All she had to do was learn the last one." He rubbed his eyes. They were starting to tear. He cleared his throat.

"I told her, Baby I love you but you must be able to say your name under duress. So I grabbed her and yelled and yelled at her till she cried and then I had her repeat her new name till she'd forgotten the old one."

I stared at him.

"Who was she?" I asked.

"Who."

"The girl whose name your daughter took."

Cigarette smoke spilled into the bar from under its courtyard door.

"Let me ask you: By whose child-slave hands were your clothes sewn? On whose backs was your home built? You don't know what atrocities you condone. Such is our compromise. We sell our own souls and other's flesh."

He was quiet. A new beer arrived.

"I suppose I know what you want," he said. "To know what kind of a man I am. If I could kidnap, could I kill." He was quiet, then, "Yes," he said, "I could do it all."

We sat there. Down the bar a man sipped whiskey with his eyes closed and music played and I remembered how Alfred had said you could become so inured to suffering that joy was dangerous—for from joy's pinnacle it was a longer descent into reality's basement.

"I want to tell you two more things about those years," he said.

"The first is the day I came home to find Maggie at our new computer. Shut it off as soon as she saw me. So that night I booted it up to sleuth only to find it'd not been the pornography I'd expected but the national kidnapped children's directory."

He reached into his pocket and pulled out an empty pack and then, "Damn," he said. "You don't smoke."

I shook my head.

"What did she find?" I asked.

"I don't know," he said. "And I don't know what made her finally suspect. Seems obvious to you and me but she didn't know anything else. Maybe it was just a hunch. Or maybe when we're young we all think we're different, special. That there's some secret we've not been let in on—that we were adopted or kidnapped or that our real parents are dead. Maybe it was from that thought that it started. And then perhaps she noticed that certain dates or stories did not align. I don't know. But in any case, it would not come up again for years."

"What was the other thing?" I asked.

He looked at me.

"You said there were two things you wanted to tell me."

He nodded. "Once my daughter came home crying. I asked her what it was and she wouldn't tell me until finally she did. Said her teacher'd called her a nigger. That's the kind of place in which we lived."

THE FATHER

♤

They live in a one story house that Maggie calls
the cabin. They eat dinner on the porch under a
bug zapper and he is amazed at how smart she's
gotten. A tree-serried sunset and grasshoppers
achirp. A cold breeze sends her in to get
sweaters. When she comes back out, they look up
and call stars by their names and theirs is a small
existence made bigger by their love.

She sips his beer and slaps at mosquitoes. He
kisses her head, embarrassing her before none
but the quiet road, the mailbox, the nocturnal
wildlife. If only he knew how much time she
spent thinking about what he'd promised to
reveal. Years of guesswork. My father the robber.
My father the kidnapper. My father the killer.
What elaborate fantasies even as she listens to
him speak, always the churning of the same
questions and evidence. What drawer has she
not rifled. If only he knew the discord he'd sewn
within. She smiles and he fills her water glass
and the sky flames with a single meteor but she
is not all there.

♤

Days weeks and months like raindrops. The milestones of adolescence too. Her first date and learning to drive and her first job and her first period long passed. It is her eighteenth birthday and she's asked for nothing—for what she wants she was promised long ago.

He is cooking in their kitchen. Stuffing, a turkey, candied sweet potatoes. It is not Thanksgiving but it is her favorite.

From the main room, with elbows propped on a checker-clothed table, she watches him.

Above the sink a window gives onto a pine hedge, a clapboard house, a dark sky in which stars shimmer like buoys. A wind chime tinkles. Savage dries his hands in a dish towel and he turns to say something but turns back round and busies himself. Neither has forgotten.

He heads into the livingroom and turns on the tv. A baseball game. He turns the volume up and stands there, his shadow harpooning the wall behind him.

"Papa," she says.

"Yes."

"Are you ready yet?"

"Almost." He heads off to his room to change his gravy-splattered shirt.

"Papa," she calls again and when he returns she is still sitting there though the television's volume is lower.

"Papa."

"I'll check on it now." He heads into the kitchen.

"No, that's not it."

He pulls a tray from the oven and burns himself and runs cold water over his hand.

"Papa."

"Yes, baby." He shuts off the faucet.

"I'm not hungry."

In the kitchen he looks at all the food and thinks about his daughter. Little to unite them but their mannerisms, their infatuation. He wonders whether he must.

"You said you'd tell me," she says.

With his back to her he shuts his eyes. Then he picks up a knife and starts carving the turkey.

"Papa, stop ignoring me."

"I'm not," he says. He fixes two plates and returns with them and sits.

"Let's say grace," he says, reaching for her hand.

"Since when?" she asks, but he lowers his head.

"God protect us," he says. "And watch over my daughter. Amen."

He takes his hand away and begins to eat.

"You have to tell me," she says.

He puts down his fork and wipes his mouth. At the end of the table is a wrapped gift.

"There are things that once known cannot be forgotten," he says.

"I know."

"Yet you ask anyway."

"Yes," she says.

"Why risk it."

"What."

"Destroying what we have."

"Papa, there's nothing you could do—"

He bangs the table. "That's not something you've tested. Life has not given you reason to hate yet. You've read and seen what people are capable of, but you've never felt it. Not even the love of a mother does not have its strings. There are fundamental prerequisites. And vice versa too. There are a great many things a parent could do to strip from them filial love."

They sit in silence. He chews and says, "Still you want to know."

She looks down at her plate, nods.

"Why," he says.

"Because," she says, her eyes glistening. She folds the edge of her napkin. But he does not wait. He begins:

"I made a decision almost eighteen years ago that has affected us daily since and under whose shadow we live. And I wish that you could feel my own heart beating in your chest so that you knew I did it from love." He looks at her. His eyes are welling. The windows are black with night.

"What did you do," she says.

"I feared for you. I thought I might come home to find you dead."

She looks at him.

"I protected you. I raised and provided for you. And you can't know what it was to come home to see your mother prepping your boiling bath in the sink. The steam rising and her face wet with tears and you screaming as though you knew that the woman who'd brought you into this world was determined to pull you out. She crying that you did not love her, that you'd been born dumb, that you'd never speak and did not recognize her and that we had to give you back for you were not hers. And she daily lying to me, telling me what I wanted to hear but her eyes and smile betraying the monologue looping within, daily the affect and thoughts more disconnected till that day she held you over the steaming water—"

"What did you—"

"I took you!" he shouted. "Jesus. I took you. To save you. I took you."

♤

He is alone. He goes out onto the porch. His breath fogs the winter air and he wears no sweater or jacket but he abides. He sits on a rickety chair, a coffee cooling in his hand. He waits. Rubs his arms. He wants to take back what he can't: If you leave now, Maggie, don't return for a year. Even then he'd wondered as he said it. A moment iterated by precedent. Life as repetition. Now he wishes she'd come home. He's not heard from her in six months and were he more like his father he'd turn to God, but his prayers have no address but the trees and the night.

♤

"Where are you going?" I asked, grabbing his arm, but he pulled me off like so much lint.

"I'll be back," he said, and once more he left.

I sat there for a moment, wanting to follow him, fearing that he would not return, but I felt woozy and the door closed his exit and he was gone. I needed to hear the ending to his story but I needed sleep more. To put my head down. To rest. I pushed off the bar and drunker than I realized stumbled to the door. The bartender called after me but I'd deal with the tab and the unfinished story in the morning. I pushed the door open into the night. It was cold and I shivered but the next thing I knew I was waking up.

The sidewalk was hard and my arm was asleep. Drool pooled on the cement. The bar was still open and my head pounded and my mouth was pasty. I pushed myself up. Car headlights telescoped by. I looked round but couldn't find my bag. I headed back in.

Savage sat there like he'd never left. He

pushed out a stool.

"Thought you were done for the night," he said.

"Thought you left," I mumbled.

"To find cigarettes," he said. He pushed a glass toward me.

I pushed it back.

"It's water," he said. "Drink it."

♤

One day he is in the livingroom reading when a knock comes. Curious to his build and demeanor he sits with crossed legs. He thinks he's hearing things, yet the knock comes again. It's been three years.

He marks his page and places his book on a side table. His knees ache from the sitting and from his work and without thinking he turns the lamp off and heads toward the door in darkness. Old carpet pads his footsteps. He opens the door. A warm and clear night.

"Hello, sir," says a young man, thin and long-haired and with holes in his jeans.

"Yes," says Savage. He places a hand on the door jamb.

"Is ... Is ..." he stutters. "Is Maggie home?"

Savage looks at the boy, then he looks up the road.

"Where is she," he says.

"Who," says the boy.

"Maggie," says Savage. The boy goes white.

"Where is she."

"I ... I ... I don't know, sir. I ... came to ... to ... to say hello. We ... we ... we ..."

"We what!" Savage shouts.

"We ... we ... we go to school ..." He steps backward.

"Where!"

"At, at, at, at ..." but it is a long time before he can speak.

THE FATHER

♤

His eyes were closed and his face glew by a
candle the bartender had placed before him.
Shadows bandied. He clasped his hands like he
was praying and he leaned his forehead atop
them and perhaps he was.

"I hadn't seen her in three years," he said.
"And this kid shows up on the anniversary of her
departure to tell me where she is. Just like that."
He wiped an eye and cleared his throat and
stared at his empty beer.

"She'd gone but stayed close. Like the
runaway in her own backyard. Or like me.
Genetics just the passing on of experience, a
repetition. That's all. And those three years her
absence stung but it was what I'd done that ate at
me like rust. The pain I'd imposed on another.
Sarah. Dear God. Like my mind's vault had
opened on a decision already justified to return it
with opposite conclusion—that I oughtn't've
done it. Jesus. That boy arriving carrying the
Trojan horse of my undoing. So overcome I
wanted to call Sarah to tell her I'd found our

daughter. Don't worry, she's back. Imagining a joyful reception though knowing the sorrow and anger and retribution to come but still holding the receiver with so many numbers dialed and only a few to go."

He sat looking at the far windows. The gold-dust light of streetlamps.

"I went to see her."

"Sarah?" I asked.

He looked at me like he'd forgotten my presence.

"Maggie," he said. "I went to see Maggie."

But in that moment, I wondered how long he'd rehearsed his story, how many times he'd practiced it, and I asked him what I hadn't until then dared:

"Do you consider yourself evil?"

A vein embossed his forehead and his eyes narrowed.

"I did my best."

I thought he'd say no more, but then he continued: "But over the years," he said, "as the threat to my daughter subsided, so too did the righteousness. I'd stripped a mother of her child. Had aimed for greatness at the cost of my soul. And for a long time I was able to busy myself with life's tribulations and that lowest common denominator, money, as a panacea to my conscience—"

"Stop it," I said.

He glared at me.

"What."

"You ..." I gathered courage. "You love the

sound of your own voice."

He was silent.

"You think the way you talk diminishes your guilt."

He looked away and then he looked at his tattooed arm and he picked at something that was not there. Then, "I am evil," he said. "May God forgive me."

♤

A small college set in a forest. Manicured lawns. Cherry blossoms. A bespectacled professor reading in the shade of a monument and Savage walking along a path. He looks up at the pediment of a building and wishes he'd chosen differently. But he knows this was never meant for him. He walks on.

The dorm is long and three stories tall and he knows which window is hers. It's not the first time he's come, but it is the first time he will enter. He is dressed in slacks and an ironed shirt covers his tattoo. He knocks on the building's door and then he bangs and then he pushes and it opens.

He knows the building but, till now, not the hallway's dank smell—smoke and antiseptic and beer—nor its adornments. Posters for clubs and rallies. Bedroom doors taped with photos and glitter and construction paper. He smiles sadly.

He heads up the stairs and passes students but none bother him and he exits on the top floor. A waxed hallway reflecting a bright sun.

The din of stereos. He knows her schedule, had surprised himself by how much he could learn with a phone call to the registrar. Now he is here.

He paces down the hallway and his new shoes squeak past rooms: 310, 311, 312, 313, 314, 315, 316. Nothing on 317's door. He listens but can hear little. He smells popcorn. Finally he knocks.

"Come in."

He stands there unmoving. His body betrays him. Perhaps his mind.

Suddenly the door opens onto a blonde girl in a sweatshirt. She is smiling and then she is not. Her face blanches.

"Maggie," she says. "Maggie."

He looks past the girl. A circle of friends watch a movie and seated on the floor is the boy he'd met months ago with his arm around his daughter.

Maggie looks up at him. Her chin quivers. There's a picture on the wall of him on the porch. A photograph he does not remember posing for.

She stands and excuses herself and does not make eye contact with him as she steps over the others to exit into the hall. She shuts the door behind her.

Her t-shirt is sleeveless and on her bicep is a dark tattoo: Mother.

Her eyes glisten and despite whatever she'd prepared she hugs him. "Papa," she says. A window at the end of the hall darkens at the passing of a cloud. She pulls away.

"I missed you," she says.

"I miss you too, baby."

He looks at her tattoo. She says nothing.

"You never came back," he says.

"I ..." Tears stream down her cheeks.

He waits and then he asks: "How've you been. How'd you get by. Did you contact her. Your mother."

He tries to wipe her face but she turns to look down the hall. They stand there quietly. The sounds of the television come muted. Someone hushing.

"Maggie," he says.

He exhales. If he stays a second longer he will bawl. He hugs her awkwardly. Her body goes limp. He looks at her for the last time and her chin is quaking but he is the one crying as he descends the stairs and she does not try to stop him.

♤

We sat there. The candle casting him in soft halo.
The thick eyebrows and the bristly chin. A man
well acquainted with labor. It was past midnight.

"What happened next," I said.

His jaw tightened. He was sweating.

"That was just two weeks ago," he said. "I saw
her once more after and it was to tell her I was
coming back here. New York City."

The light of a neon sign reflected in his eye
and he opened his hands looking at each in turn.

"My greatness has been a sham, a trick of the
ego, and it took me two decades to realize it. That
the only greatness I had within me was making
that girl. A life squandered and turned to shadow
and it will be defined by three events alone. The
best thing I ever did and the worst I done and the
bravest I am about to." He pushed away from the
bar.

"Where are you going?" I asked.

He walked away.

"Savage!" I shouted.

"Savage!"

The door opened and he left and it shut and I wanted to tell him that there was always hope, that there was always worth in our existence and greatness resided not in the large but in the minuscule—in how Alfred would cook me dinner as though for a king and in how he said goodbye and in how he listened. And even though he'd taken his own life he had still been great—to me. To me. And I did not believe in God but I prayed for him, for Alfred, and I would pray for Savage too. And I would pray for all the Savages who found no meaning in their lives and so resorted to the heinous simply to feel their own pulses, to feel like they'd done something even if all they did was pave a trail of misery. I would pray for them, me the nonbeliever who carried nothing but a small flame flapping at each heartbreak, each loss. I wanted to tell him I loved him— Alfred and Savage and all those who felt eternally passed over by the hand of fortune. I loved them, all of them, and their greatness resided not in the illustrious or notorious, but in this, our shared existence, and though I was no one, a nobody myself, I wanted to tell him that I forgave him too, that I forgave him for making this world as it was and not as it should be. I forgave him for what he'd done, all of them ...

ACKNOWLEDGMENTS

It's impossible to thank everyone who has played some role (big or small) in the making of this book, but you never know what action will be your last, so I will try.

First, I'd like to thank my family—my mother, my father, my sister, Laura, and her husband, Rodrigo, and my brother, Gabe, and his girlfriend, Steph—each of you, in your own way, has taught me love and kindness and has supported me through every single one of my madnesses (which we call books). I thank you deeply. I have to thank both my mother and father in specific: my wonderful mother for originally encouraging me to write (fifteen years ago) and my incredible father, first, for helping me to get this book out, but more so, for allowing the relationship we have now to have developed, the kind of father-son relationship that many never have but of which I have always dreamed. And to Faina, my partner, no thanks are good enough. You are amazing to me, and you are my hero. I love you. (And your family—Elvira, Alla, Rashid, Yan, Dima, Mark, and Bella.)

To my extended family in the US—Ana María, Konstantine, Alekos and his girlfriend, Vanessa —you guys have kept me anchored and infused me with countless memories. How can I thank you for all those vacations in North Carolina? For all those walks along the beach? For the number of times you've fed me and vacuumed up the cat hair before I arrived? Thank you! And to my extended family in Argentina (it seems unjust to not name any of you, but I dare not start, for with more than twenty cousins, many married and with kids, and ten uncles and aunts, I fear tremendously skipping even a single one of you), thank you for the love you have always given me, even from afar. I hope we can all reunite either here or in Argentina soon! (Especially you Mario, Carolina, Matias, Belen, Lalo, Rosi, Pablo, Julian, Lula, Martín, Fede, Augustín, Joaquín, Daniel, Viviana, Santi, Nacho, Clara, and Tancho, Liliana, Juan Pablo, Victoria, Ignacio, Verónica, Lourdes, Juanqui, and Facundo—ok, I cheated a little.)

Somehow, despite myself, I seem to have made some friends, and I'd like to thank first the friends who go back to middle school: Fred Berger, David Mait (and Francesca!), David Noah and Rachel Coleman, Michael Romano, Jacob Stevenson (and Leonie!), Tom Suharto and Jenna Williams, Aaron Vaughn, and Nick Williams and Sara Khwaja. Though we mostly got lucky with our families (in families you have no choice, but in friends you do), by maintaining our friendships over years, we've slipped from one category (friends) and into another (family), and so I feel very much bound to all of you. Thank you for these decades of friendship. To Hannah Moore and Saumil Patel—who once in a while doesn't send me to voicemail (ha! I love you)—Adam and Caitlin Cincotta—whose own relationship is older than soil (ha!)—Kristin Seeger and to the rest of my college friends who've scattered and grown busier but become no less dear—Matt Jossen, Rob and Carolyn Komorowski, Neil McQuarrie, JB and Ariel Osborne, Brett and Allison Owens, Alan and Merri Suzuki, and Rob and Ashley Willim.

Thank you to my relatively "newer" writer friends from The New School—Joy Baglio, Hassoon Hadi, Amy Kurzweil (and Jacob Sparks), Rebecca Nison, and Jesse VanDusen—and my teachers there: Bob Antoni, Susan Bell, Shelley Jackson, Jackson Taylor, and Stephen Wright. A particularly warm thank you to my thesis advisor Tiphanie Yanique for supporting me through this difficult game we call writing, to my one-time agent Priya Doraswamy for taking a chance on me, and to Claudia Yelin for allowing me to edit her novel. To the friends I've made through teaching and tutoring (some lifelong!)—Isaac Foster, Rich Joseph, Brian Leibowitz (now it's your turn!), Tim Levin, James and Sarah Milana, Frank Queris, and Sandyrose Rolon—and to the New York City friends I've made along the way: Neema Atri, Mehdi Omidvar and Soha Gholitabar, Mina Markham, Sam Shapiro, and Ross Weythman. A big thank you also to my even newer Philadelphia friends—Andrew, Bhumika, Bill, Elijah, Joe Varsanyi and St. Michael's, John, Josh Brechter, Josh Martin (and Nikki!), Yuki, Rodney, Ross Boone (yes, I'm trying to get you to move), Sam, Shingo, and Sydney—and to Sensei Jason Perna and the rest of the Old City Aikido crew. Thank you for welcoming me into your home.

An incredibly big thank you to Israel Molina without whose spark no one would be reading these words.

Thank you to our old family friends: the Kalinecs, the Cohens, the Malosowskis, the Castillo-Trujillos, and the Politis.

And, finally, a tremendous thank you to Sensei Ryūgan Savoca for teaching me more than I can ever repay you for and to the dojo and community you and Kate (and Cormac!) have built. Thank you to Brooklyn Aikikai, to the brothers and sisters forged there—Spencer "I'm Done" Cobrin, Nikki Calonge, Mike Croes (and Rebecca!), Noah Landes, Krissie Nagy, Aaron Taber, Haryo Shridhar, Donny Donahue, Sarah Kaylor, Sean MacNintch, Kortney Barber, Martine Baruch, Rebecca Scheckman, Andrew Wilder, Sam and Max Geller, James Yagaeshi, Scott Ashen, Damien Scott, Lorenzo Tijerina (and Tania!), Joon Pyo Lee, Bethany Martin, Justin and Jenny Coletti, Anne Toomey, Rui Totani, Lucy Clark, Alan Rodriguez Penney,

Jacques Aboaf, Zuihō Perez, Patrick Manian, Dinos Tsambounieris, Jason Gerlak, Billy Donahue, Patric Dovicak, Harmony Eberhardt, Sami Elderazi, Akira Fukui, Chase Girvin, Pinny Grunwald, David Laufer, Zachary Ludescher, Spencer Lum, Joanna Mattrey, Diego Rosas, Colin Nusbaum, Elana Redfield, Leonard Rutkowitz, Julina Tatlock, Melissa Valencia, Adam Sorkin—and the rest of my fellow aikidoka, too many to name, but each of whom I have learned greatly from. I thank all of you. Thank you as well to the teachers who have both made me struggle and seen me through it: Hiruta Sensei, Komyo Seido, Boyet Sensei, Piotr Sensei, Roo Heins Sensei, Lyons Sensei, and the many other teachers who have helped (and continue to help) me along the way.

And, really lastly, this book is one of love and loss; thank you to all my old loves, lusts, crushes, and passions who perhaps I best not name, but who remain in my memory. Thank you, all of you, and if I have forgotten anyone, forgive me— if you really know me, you know my memory's a sieve. Ok, that's enough!

ABOUT THE AUTHOR

After graduating from Cornell, Andrés Cruciani earned a Master's in Education from Brooklyn College and an MFA from The New School. He has been a teacher for 15 years and has taught writing at FIT and the Hispanic Center for Excellence at Albert Einstein College among other places. He has had numerous pieces nominated for awards and published in *The Westchester Review, Pamplemousse, Green Mountain Review,* and *Welter* among other magazines. He served as editor for LIT magazine, is the current senior editor of Brooklyn Aikikai Journal, and recently founded Toho Publishing. When not writing, Andrés trains in Aikido. *The Father* is his first published book.

You can find more here:
www.andrescruciani.com.